D0193471

THE ANCIENT OCEAN BLUES

THE ANCIENT OCEAN BLUES

JACK MITCHELL

Tundra Books

Text copyright © 2008 by Jack Mitchell

Published in Canada by Tundra Books,
75 Sherbourne Street, Toronto, Ontario M5A 2P9

Published in the United States by Tundra Books of Northern New York,
P.O. Box 1030, Plattsburgh, New York 12901

Library of Congress Control Number: 2007943133

All rights reserved. The use of any part of this publication
reproduced, transmitted in any form or by any means, electronic,
mechanical, photocopying, recording, or otherwise, or stored
in a retrieval system, without the prior written consent of the
publisher – or, in case of photocopying or other reprographic copying,
a licence from the Canadian Copyright Licensing Agency – is an
infringement of the copyright law.

Library and Archives Canada Cataloguing in Publication

Mitchell, Jack, 1977-
The ancient ocean blues / Jack Mitchell.

ISBN 978-0-88776-832-3

I. Title.

PS8626.I838A65 2008   jC813'.6   C2007-907602-5

We acknowledge the financial support of the Government of Canada
through the Book Publishing Industry Development Program (BPIDP)
and that of the Government of Ontario through the Ontario Media
Development Corporation's Ontario Book Initiative. We further
acknowledge the support of the Canada Council for the Arts and the
Ontario Arts Council for our publishing program.

ONTARIO ARTS COUNCIL
CONSEIL DES ARTS DE L'ONTARIO

Cover Design: Terri Nimmo

Printed and bound in Canada

This book is printed on acid-free paper that is 100% recycled,
ancient-forest friendly (40% post-consumer recycled).

1 2 3 4 5 6   13 12 11 10 09 08

for
Margaret Mitchell
my mother

Characters

Marcus	(Marcus Oppius Sabinus) The Narrator
Gaius	(Gaius Oppius Sabinus) Older cousin of Marcus's, associate of Julius Caesar's
Caesar	(Julius Caesar) Up-and-coming politician in Rome
Cicero	Consul of Rome, rival of Julius Caesar
Pompey	(Pompey the Great) Roman Admiral, rival of Julius Caesar
Paulla	(Aemilia Lepida Paulla) Aristocratic Roman girl, betrothed to Marcus
Tullia, Fulvia, Spurius	Friends of Marcus's and Paulla's in Rome
Spurinna	(Aulus Lucinus Spurinna) Young man from Etruria, friend of Cicero's
The Captain	Carthaginian merchant, captain of the *Star of Carthage*
Homer	(Aulus Lucinus Homerus) Greek publisher and freedman of Spurinna's
Brasidas	Exiled Spartan landowner in Laconia
Anaxilaus	Greek philosopher in Athens
Atticus	Roman knight, resident in Athens, and close friend of Cicero's

Contents

Bread for Caesar

No one in Rome could bribe you like my cousin Gaius. He was the greatest briber in the City, and that's saying quite a lot.

"Marcus, my lad," he declared, when I first went to live with him, "you've come here at the right time. This is the Golden Age of Bribery. Corruption is rife. The Republic of Rome is crumbling. You stick with me. You'll learn all you need to know."

I wasn't much more than a boy at the time, and I had just come of age. My parents had noticed how bored I was with life in Reate, our little town in the Sabine country, which was very perceptive of them, so they sent me off to live in the City with Gaius. Gaius was actually my father's second cousin but, as far as my parents were concerned, he was family: a successful lawyer, a friend of Senators and Judges, an admirer of poetry, and overall just the right person to show a young fellow how Rome worked. What they didn't know was that he was also the most cynical person in Italy.

Gaius's job was to buy elections. Of course, he didn't put it like that. In his own eyes, he was merely helping Rome achieve its destiny, or something. In any case, once a month a heavy chest full of treasure – ten slaves could barely lift it – would arrive on his doorstep and Gaius would personally wrap the money up in discreet little bundles, covered with linen cloth, and quietly deliver those bundles to influential voters. He called the process "politics," and he loved it.

Gaius had just started working for Julius Caesar. Everyone would come to know that name in time, of course, but in those days, Caesar was no more than a young Temple-keeper with a lot of ambition. Naturally, most young Temple-keepers are ambitious: you can't get much lower, as a magistrate, than looking after temples and sewers, so there's nowhere to go but up. But Caesar was aiming for the stars, even if he was young and poor and despised by the nobles. To get ahead, he had turned to people like my cousin Gaius.

"Caesar is my kind of politician," Gaius would often remark, as he relaxed in the garden at the end of a hard day of bribing. "No qualms, no dithering, no invoking the glory of the ancestors: just cold hard cash. Mark my words, lad, Caesar is our future."

So indeed it seemed. With help from Gaius and others

like him, Caesar was on the rise. With no money of his own, he borrowed left and right, and then he spent it all on politics – a magnificent gladiator show here, an expensive wedding there. He was making a name for himself, and the people noticed. Still, everyone was amazed when he chose to run in the election for High Priest of Rome. That lifelong post always went to an old aristocrat, since it was the most important religious office in the Republic: the High Priest looked after the Divine Law, a very complex subject, and was the final authority on the Will of the Gods. Not exactly a job for an impoverished thirty-seven-year-old Temple-keeper. But nothing scared Caesar and Gaius. This time they got serious, and the borrowing and the bribing reached unheard-of levels.

That was how I got involved.

It was about noon, in the summer before the election for High Priest. I was at home after school, pacing up and down the front hall as I tried to memorize a speech. I was going to recite it in class the next day. Suddenly, Gaius burst through the front door. He was alone, which was strange: usually half a dozen of his gang would be hanging round. He came straight up to me.

"Marcus!" he cried. "Stop talking to yourself like that, it makes you look like the village idiot. Listen, we need your help!"

"What's that?" I asked, breaking off my speech. "Where's the gang?"

"They're all off delivering packages. We're shorthanded. I need you to take something to the Roman Market." He handed me a letter sealed in red wax and gave me the name of a Roman knight. A tall fellow, he said, with curly hair.

"What is this?" I asked.

"Obviously, it's a letter," Gaius replied sharply. "You deliver it and make sure the knight reads it. Then come back and report what he says. Quick now!"

I put on my sandals and my new toga in a rush and hurried down to the Roman Market, which wasn't far off. It was one of those incredibly hot August days when the citizens all retreat to the deep shade of the colonnades, and the slaves are busy fanning everybody. I found my Roman knight sitting on a bench, alone. The edge of his toga was dirty and he looked depressed.

"Pardon me," I said, "but I think I have something for you."

He looked up without a word, and took the letter as a matter of course. When he saw who it was from, however, he scowled.

"This is from Gaius Oppius?"

I said it was.

The knight finished reading, but said nothing. He stared across the sun-baked Market.

"Can he have it ready by tomorrow?" he asked at last.

I hesitated. I had no idea what he was talking about. But

Gaius did seem in a rush and he always had lots of everything.

"Of course he can," I replied.

The knight stood up and looked me over. He noticed my bright new toga and it seemed to depress him. But he managed a smile.

"Does this get me alone, or does it include my brothers too?" he inquired.

Again I had no idea. I picked one answer. I wanted to return home and practice my speech.

"Your brothers too," I said, as firmly as I could.

The knight seemed disappointed, but he put the letter carefully away.

"Give my greetings to Gaius Oppius and tell him he can count on us," he said, and walked off quickly.

Back home, I made my report to Gaius. He was writing at his desk. In the corner, the secretary was also scribbling away like mad.

"Marcus! Did you deliver the letter?" Gaius demanded. "What did he say?"

I told him.

"Good, good, that's another knight we've got." He smiled. "And for only five gold pieces! Old Roman family, you see, and worth a lot more than that when the voting starts. Now we just need to see about his brothers –"

"Oh no," I broke in, "I told him it *included* his brothers."

Gaius dropped his pen. The secretary stopped scribbling and looked up.

"You said *that*?" cried Gaius. "And he agreed? You mean – *do* you mean the whole clan is voting with us? For just five gold pieces? Marcus, the man has six brothers! How? How did you do that?" He seemed torn between shock at my boldness and admiration for the result.

"Well, I just looked him in the eye, you know," I mumbled. "It seemed like he needed your help."

My cousin grinned. "That's right, he does, doesn't he? But to get the whole clan! Well, well, you sized him up." He took a deep breath and walked me to the garden at the back of the house.

"I've been overlooking you, Marcus," he began. "Never thought a lad like you from Reate could make a politician, but you seem to have an instinct for it." He rubbed his hands with satisfaction. "You've been keeping your eyes open, eh? Just like I predicted."

I never did deliver that speech in class, because the next day Gaius informed me that I was no longer going to school and would now be working for Julius Caesar.

"Believe me, you'll pick up more doing this anyway," he claimed. "Giving speeches, writing letters, geography, the law – you speak Greek, don't you?"

I said yes, quite well. I'd had a Greek nurse when I was small.

"Good, that's a big asset. Do you like bread?"

Bread, it transpired, was my new job. That is, I spent the next month delivering bread around the City. Every morning, Gaius's slaves would pile two dozen loaves of it into a hand-cart; after that, one of Gaius's gang, a rather scrawny person from the outskirts, would push the cart through various neighborhoods while I walked in front and did the talking. Gaius made me memorize where to go and how many loaves to give each customer. I was supposed to bow, hand over the bread, and say, "With the compliments of Caesar." The cart-pusher would wait nervously in the street while I made my deliveries.

Looking back, I suppose I was a bit naive. For the first ten days I couldn't understand what this wretched bread had to do with politics or Julius Caesar or anyone being High Priest of Rome, and I wished I was back in school. Nevertheless, the whole operation was suspicious. For starters, the scrawny cart-pusher was constantly peeping over his shoulder, even when I was with him. At the end of each day he would mop his brow, slap me on the back, and exclaim, "Home again, safe and sound! Thank the gods!"

Then there was the fact that, even though the bread was black, heavy, coarse-grained, and unappetizing, our customers always greeted me with huge enthusiasm. They would shake my hand, thank me heartily, and send the loaves back to their kitchens right away. Some of them

even wanted to drink my health, though our busy sched-
ule rarely allowed time for it.

Finally, it seemed that the wealthier you were, the more
of the horrible bread you ordered. One old gentleman was
even disappointed that he couldn't get an extra loaf, and
he kept eyeing the cart hungrily as I said good-bye.

I could have asked Gaius, of course. But he was so
pleased with me that, after the first few days of bread delivery, I didn't want to let on that I had no idea what I was
doing. In the end, I didn't find out how deeply involved in
his schemes I really was, until I nearly got arrested.

It was the end of a long morning of pushing the cart
uphill (for I helped out on the steep slopes), and I was vis-
iting my third customer of the day. I forget the Senator's
name, but he had a large and rather run-down mansion
at the top of the Esquiline Hill. As usual, I left the cart-
pusher in the street. I was so worn out, however, that I
somehow forgot to bring the loaves of bread inside.

In the front hall, the Senator was there waiting for me.
He wasn't alone. A rather ordinary-looking man, with a
round head and graying hair, was arguing with him. I
didn't need the thick purple edge of his toga to tell me who
he was: Cicero, the Consul of Rome, the highest magistrate
in the City. He was flanked by two bodyguards, each one
holding an ax. He and the Senator seemed on the point of
raising their voices just as I walked in.

Noticing me, they fell silent. Cicero gave me a hostile smile. Then he turned squarely back to the Senator.

"Well, now. Precisely who might your guest be, exactly? A friend of Julius Caesar? A friend of Gaius Oppius?"

The Senator was looking at me with horror. I bowed politely.

"My name is Marcus Oppius Sabinus," I began. "I'm sorry to interrupt. I'm just here with the bread delivery."

The Senator was trembling visibly.

"Ah yes, the bread!" exclaimed Cicero triumphantly. "Five days till the election, and you've come about the bread. I see. Well, aren't you going to deliver it?"

Only then did I notice I had left the bread back in the cart. I stuttered a quick apology, and the Senator looked relieved. I started back toward the door.

"Just a moment," said Cicero in a booming voice. "Guards, I think we will all accompany this young man outside – you too, Senator – and we will see just what sort of bread Julius Caesar has sent the Senator today."

At last, I realized something was terribly wrong: the frightened Senator, the gleam in the Consul's eye, the very broad shoulders of the bodyguards carrying their axes. I suddenly felt sick. What had Gaius gotten me into? There was nothing to do but shuffle out into the street behind Cicero. When the Consul makes a suggestion, he expects to be obeyed.

"I can only think of five laws against corruption, Senator," he was saying bitterly as we emerged from the house, "but I promise that the guilty will answer to every one of them, of that you may be sure. It is too early to speak of fines, or exile, but you understand that justice must – Now, where is your bread, young man?"

This last was directed to me, most impatiently. Cicero was looking left and right, and our eyes followed his. But the street was deserted. I had left the cart-pusher and our cart, which was quite full, loitering under the shade of a fruit tree, not ten paces off. There was no sign of them now. We stood together awkwardly for some moments in silence. Cicero's face was turning deep red.

"It was just here!" I protested at last. "There was a cart, and my assistant!"

"Oh, there was, was there?" said Cicero. "Well, your cart and your assistant have vanished, and your wonderful bread's gone with them! Very convenient, isn't it?"

"I don't know where he's gone, I tell you! Anyway, it's just a bit of harmless bread!"

"Of course, of course," answered Cicero, grinning through clenched teeth. "Harmless to everyone but the Republic of Rome." He swallowed hard. He was on the point of losing his dignity, his most precious possession, and it infuriated him. "Well," he said, "I can only declare that you – both of you – should thank heaven. Don't think

I don't know what happened here, Senator. You may be safe today, but I won't forget. And you, young man, give my greetings to Gaius Oppius, and tell him his bread is getting stale."

With that, he stalked off with his bodyguards. The Senator called a hasty good-bye and fled back into his disheveled mansion. I was left alone to catch my breath. As there was still no sign of the cart-pusher, I adjusted my toga and began walking back to Gaius's house.

At the first intersection, however, the cart-pusher magically reappeared. His eyes were staring wide.

"Are they gone? Are they gone?" he babbled at me.

"You mean the Consul? Yes, he left."

"Thank the gods! Thank the blessed, immortal gods! I was sure you were done for, sir. I saw the guards through the door when you went in and I legged it!"

"Where is the cart?"

He led me to a back alley, where the cart, piled with random bits of garbage, was hidden. I wasted no time. I seized a loaf and took a bite. At once, my tooth struck something hard inside, and I pulled the lump out of my mouth. It was a bit sticky, but it gleamed.

"Gold," I said dully. I had tasted a small gold coin.

"Yessir, the silver was last month," the cart-pusher put in. "I think it's going to be gems soon, before they start voting."

I put the bread back and stared at the coin in my hand. I was shaking. How far had I gone in personally undermining the Roman State? Why had I ever left Reate? How many millions had I been dispersing?

"Just enough," Gaius said later on that evening in answer to my question. "Or so we hope. Otherwise it could get a bit expensive. Can you believe how much a jury costs to bribe these days?" He seemed to think my encounter with Cicero was very funny.

"But he knows," I insisted. "Cicero knows. He's the Consul of Rome!"

"Don't worry, Marcus," Gaius answered soothingly. "Caesar will win, and he'll keep on winning. This is only the beginning. They're already talking about you as a dedicated Caesar supporter. He'll protect us all."

"What if Caesar *doesn't* win?"

"Well, there's always the chance to travel. Spain, maybe. You know, a fresh start."

"*Exile?*"

"Try and look on the bright side. Chances are, you'll soon be friends with the High Priest of Rome. It's as simple as that. The Will of the Gods."

Terrific, I thought. *Here's to the bright side, and here's to the Will of the Gods.*

The Mission to Greece

Of course, Caesar won. He beat the most pious and respected old man in the City for the job, and suddenly Rome had a thirty-seven-year-old Temple-keeper as its High Priest. The Senate was shocked, but what could they do? It was too late to buy the election back.

Needless to say, Gaius was ecstatic. He hosted the grand victory banquet, and Caesar himself, the guest of honor, shook my hand afterwards.

"Thank you, Marcus Oppius," he said. "You are worthy of your loyal cousin."

Meanwhile, Rome nearly had a revolution. For once, this had nothing to do with Gaius. A desperate aristocrat, named Catiline, put together a Conspiracy against the Republic, recruiting unhappy nobles and disgruntled old soldiers. They planned to massacre the entire Senate, seize the public treasury, and bring in barbarians to plunder Rome. Or so we heard. It all happened quickly. The first thing we knew about it was when Cicero, who was the greatest orator in Rome, denounced Catiline in the Senate and drove him and his conspirators from the City. Then the Roman Army marched out to fight Catiline's forces. There was a terrific battle up North, Catiline was killed, and the Roman Republic survived. Cicero's prestige soared sky-high, and they voted him the title of Father of his Country.

Thankfully, I watched all this from the cheap seats. I was in the crowd when they drove Catiline through the city gates, but I never laid eyes on the man himself. That was fine with me: I'm not the hero type.

The strangest thing about the whole affair, however, was the mysterious role played by a young man from the country, Aulus Lucinus Spurinna. The story was hard to get straight, but apparently he had traveled to Rome from his home in Etruria just in time to help foil the Conspiracy. The rumor in the Market was that he was the real reason for Cicero's success, and since he was almost exactly my age I was often asked if I knew him. Fortunately, I did not, though my friends reported several "Spurinna sightings" all through that winter.

It was Gaius, as you might expect, who got me mixed up with it. He was breathing easily once again, after the end of the Conspiracy. For a while he had been sure the conspirators would murder him and take his money, but once it was over he got back to business – in his case, the business of getting Caesar's friends elected. Myself, I had gone

back to school, since I missed reading my speeches in front
of the class; so I was surprised when Gaius kept me after
dinner one winter evening, sending away the servants so
that we could talk in private.

He got to the point. "Look here, young Marcus, it's time
you came out of retirement."

I reminded him that I was in school, not retirement.

"That's what I mean," he said. "You showed what you
could do during the election. Now you're wasting your
time in school. What about your career?"

I pointed out that my career so far had involved wholesale bribery.

"Your career," Gaius answered primly, "involved
nothing of the sort. Not wholesale, anyway. You haven't
seen wholesale yet. But this is different. We need you to
find out some information. What do you know about
Pompey?"

"You mean the Admiral? Pompey the Great?"

Gaius frowned. "Well, some people call him 'the Great.'
Not us, though. He's Julius Caesar's biggest rival. He's
trying to dominate Rome."

"Aren't *we* trying to dominate Rome?" I asked.

"Exactly! Which is why we have to stop Pompey. You're
finally talking sense. Well, as you know, at the moment he's
Admiral of the Mediterranean, and he's off in Greece fighting pirates. We were the ones who got him the command
of the fleet – to get rid of him."

"So what's the problem?"

"The problem is that he's about to come back. They say he's almost finished destroying the pirates, and then he'll return to Rome in triumph. But we must prevent him from corrupting the Republic!"

I couldn't believe Gaius said that with a straight face.

"Now then," he went on, "Pompey is thinking of joining forces, politically, with that fellow Cicero. What do you think of that?" he asked, eyeing me.

I said they could be quite a combination: Cicero's powerful voice and Pompey's military glory.

"It would be disastrous!" Gaius cried. "They would block our every move. And yet," – here he leaned forward with a twinkle in his eye – "our spies have found out the critical detail. We know the name of the person Cicero is going to send to Greece to meet Pompey this spring. You'll never guess. It's that young man Aulus Lucinus Spurinna, the one who stopped the Conspiracy."

Somehow, even then, I felt my heart sink.

"Your job," Gaius continued happily, "is to talk to this Spurinna and find out – discreetly, mind you – what Cicero and Pompey are up to, and when exactly Spurinna leaves for Greece. Just talk to him."

"I've never met Spurinna," I said.

"You will. You're invited to a party tomorrow night. Spurinna will be there."

"A party? Me? How did you manage that?" I demanded.

"Easy," said Gaius, with a grin. "The party is at Paulla's house."

Why I didn't walk out then and there, I don't know. Paulla was one of my least favorite people in the City. Unfortunately my parents had arranged for me to marry her. Her family was ancient and powerful, and it was my father's principal joy in life that I would someday be linked to the clan of the Aemilii through Paulla. Of course, the wedding (if it ever happened) was still years away, but in the meantime I had to be extremely nice to Paulla whenever I saw her. My solution was to see her as rarely as possible. She was pretty enough, but her idea of a good book was a Greek romance novel, and she was always trying to get her friends to read them. Fortunately she didn't think much of me, either.

I would ordinarily have refused to go, but Gaius was a hard man to say "No" to. Steadily, he proved that I was the only man for the job: the usual spies would never blend in. And Caesar would be extremely grateful. And the food would be terrific. And everyone would be looking their best. And so on.

At last, I said "Yes," just to get it over with. Then I went to my room and practiced a speech for school.

I spent the next morning and early afternoon getting ready. If I was going to go to the party, I would do it right. First I went to the barber and got my hair trimmed in the

Spanish style, very short, which made me look older. The barber did an excellent job. Unfortunately, he sang sentimental Campanian love songs the whole time. After I escaped from his shop, I glanced at the sun and saw it was still too early for the public bath – they opened the doors at the seventh hour – so I went down to the Roman Market to look for a new shirt. It was nice to have some spending money, thanks to my work for Gaius, and I picked a red one with a blue stripe and embroidered Greek trim. My next stop was back near Gaius's house, by the gardens, where they sold head-garlands; I would have to bring one to Paulla's party. They were quite expensive, and the variety made it hard to choose: myrtle, ivy, or parsley. I thought the ivy would make me look like an old wall, and I baulked at wearing anything edible, so I chose myrtle.

"And would the young gentleman care to select a flower for his crown?" the garland-seller inquired.

"No," I answered firmly, "the young gentleman would not."

I left the new shirt and the manly myrtle garland at Gaius's house and then I headed for the baths. It was February. The wind was cold, I wanted to soak in the hot pool. I got there just as the gong sounded, signaling that the bath was open. I managed to get inside and underwater before the crowds came in. The heat did me good. I skipped the plunge into the cold pool since the air outside was just as invigorating.

At home I took a nap. When I awoke, I found that the slaves had washed, dried, and ironed my toga and polished my sandals. I put on my shirt, and they helped me into the toga. Finally, Gaius's old nurse adjusted the garland on my head and I set forth, borrowing the sedan-chair so I wouldn't get my toga dirty.

The sun was just setting when I reached Paulla's house. Braziers were flaming merrily outside the front door. I descended from the sedan-chair and strode inside.

"Marcus Oppius Sabinus," the herald proclaimed, as I stepped across the threshold, past the long portrait gallery of the Aemilii ancestors, and into the brightly lit front hall.

As I looked round, I had to admit that Paulla had done a nice job. Everything looked just as it would look for a party of adults: the guests were wearing their head-garlands, and there was lots of fine food, with a light wine to drink. The only difference was the height of the guests, since this was a party for young people. No one seemed to be more than eighteen, and most were my age. I recognized my friend Spurius, and there was Fulvia, and Tullia. I would be all right. People were standing in groups and there was a band in the corner playing background music – when your clan is the Aemilii, you can afford to own a band. In fact, the entire scene almost looked like as much fun as Gaius had imagined.

I joined the circle with Spurius and Fulvia and another young man I didn't know, but straightaway the hostess appeared.

"Marcus!" said Paulla, sliding into our group and taking Fulvia by the arm. "My mother said you would turn up. Are you here to bribe us?" she asked with a laugh. She was dressed like a queen, her dark hair in ringlets.

"Marcus was just about to offer us a piece of his bread," said Fulvia, joining in.

I blushed.

"The famous bread?" Paulla went on. "I hear it's quite tasty. Baked by High Priest Caesar himself, isn't that right?"

"Of course, Paulla," exclaimed Fulvia, "wouldn't it go perfectly with the grilled golden trout?"

I cut in at last.

"No bread tonight," I managed to get out, with a rasp.

"No bread?" said the young man I had not met, with a puzzled look. He had a slight accent. "Why, back home in Etruria, we always have bread with our meal."

I waited for Paulla to crush this feeble remark mercilessly, but instead she just widened her eyes at the young man and said, "Oh, Etruria! Is that where you fought the battle, Aulus?"

She was so absorbed in the stranger that she never

introduced him, but I put two and two together neatly – battle, Etruria, and the name *Aulus* – and realized at once that the young man Paulla was staring at could only be Aulus Lucinus Spurinna. He was taller than I was, and well-built, and he had wavy brown hair. His shirt and toga were simple, but he stood up very straight.

"Well, it wasn't just me," he said simply. "I played a small part. All I did was charge with the cavalry."

Paulla wouldn't tolerate such self-effacement. "They say it was your charge that killed the enemy general!" she exclaimed.

Spurinna shrugged. "Right place at the right time, I guess."

The girls sighed with admiration at his modesty, and even my cynical friend Spurius looked impressed. Paulla, in particular, appeared to be about to faint.

"It's just like in the novel, *The Sicilian Story*," she gasped, "when the hero saves the city in the last chapter. One of the best novels there is. You've read it, haven't you?" she asked Spurinna eagerly.

Fortunately, the bell for supper saved us, or else Spurinna would doubtless have recited the book from memory. I was already finding him a bit much. His Etrurian accent grated on the ears.

At the table, Spurinna lay down on the couch of honor, and I was nearby. Somehow Gaius had taken care of that. Paulla was facing Spurinna. Apparently she herself had taken care of that. When the waiters brought us bread, I steeled myself for another round of wit.

"Maybe there's a secret inside!"

"I already feel like voting for Caesar!"

As the laughter died down, Spurinna, who was still looking puzzled, turned to me.

"What on earth are they talking about?" he asked.

"Oh, well, yes, that: it's about religion," I stammered. "The ancient bread rituals, you know. Very special. You probably don't have them in Etruria."

"What Marcus means, Aulus," said Paulla, intervening, "is that corruption is rife in the Republic."

"Corruption?" asked Spurinna in surprise.

"Right," she went on, rolling her eyes at me. "Some people think they can buy elections."

"Buy? Buy an election?" Spurinna cried, shocked. "In Rome? That couldn't happen!" He turned to me. "Marcus Oppius, have you heard of such a thing? You seem like someone who understands the City. Could it happen, in Rome?"

Was he making fun of me? I growled that anything was possible in these degenerate times.

"But free and fair elections are what made Rome great!" Spurinna went on. "Cicero often says so. Surely no one would tarnish the name of Rome like that!"

"Doesn't it happen in Etruria?" I asked wearily.

"Bribery? Never!"

Apparently Spurinna wasn't making fun of me; he was either stupid, or incredibly naive. I tried to change the subject.

"Do you often speak with Cicero?" I inquired.

He said yes. He was often at Cicero's house, and was friends with Tullia, Cicero's daughter. She was at another table, and Spurinna glanced in her direction. But he sighed.

"She's getting married soon," he said sadly. "To an aristocrat. It's politics. She says she doesn't like him, much."

"Oh, these arranged marriages!" Paulla exclaimed with feeling. She gave me a sour look and put her hand on Spurinna's arm. "I know how it is, Aulus, believe me. Can you guess who my parents have set me up with? With Marcus here! Isn't that incredible?"

I remarked that we were all at the mercy of the gods.

"It doesn't matter," Spurinna said, doing his best impersonation of a Roman hero overcome with grief, "because I am going out East. Cicero himself is sending me."

"To Alexandria?" I prompted him.

"No, to Athens, in Greece," he said, as though there were several Athenses. "I'm off to join Pompey and the fleet. They're fighting pirates, and I want to do my duty."

"How romantic!" said Paulla. "It's just like in the novel, *The Tale of Two Nobles*, when they fight the Pirate King."

"When do you leave?" I asked.

"Tomorrow morning," Spurinna answered. "On a fast warship. I stayed tonight because I wanted one last chance to see Tull –"

"Tomorrow!" interrupted Paulla, astonished. "But, Aulus, you can't leave tomorrow! I was sure you would be with us another month! You can't go so soon!"

"Now, now," I said. "I'm sure our Etrurian friend is keen to get out to where the plunder is."

"Indeed I am," he replied, mistaking my meaning. "The Cilician pirates have been plundering the coasts for too long. They're fierce, and they're fearless, and it's time we stood up to them."

"Like Caesar did," I put in. "You know the story, I'm sure. He was no older than we are now, and the pirates captured him at sea. They wanted to ransom him, of course, but he told them they should kill him directly, because if they ransomed him he would track them down."

"And what happened?"

"They ransomed him. He tracked them down. And he crucified them all."

"Marcus," said Paulla severely, after a pause. "Don't be ridiculous. That would make a very horrible novel."

Next morning, I reported to Gaius.

"Spurinna is definitely going to Greece," I confirmed. "But you must be wrong about him. He's not a political agent. He's, well" – I searched for the right words – "he's completely witless."

"Don't be silly, Marcus," Gaius said gently. "That's all an act. Believe me, he's one of the cleverest agents in the City. Look what he did to Catiline! And they say he's a bit of a hero. Did you ask him about the battle?"

"It's irrelevant," I went on, "because you're too late, anyway. He's going to join Pompey and he sailed this morning on a warship."

"What? This morning!" cried Gaius, jumping out of his chair. "You can't be serious! It's February. The sailing season isn't until April!" He was suddenly panicking.

"That wouldn't matter to Spurinna," I said wearily. "He'd probably enjoy a storm or two. They'd give him a chance to do his duty."

"But – but – we have to stop him!" Gaius was pacing the room now, holding his hair. "Cicero and Pompey – no! We have to . . ."

Suddenly he stopped. Slowly he turned around, his eyes gleaming wickedly.

"Absolutely not!" I roared. "I won't go!"

"You have to follow him, Marcus. Follow him to Greece. Keep him away from Pompey. Take a ship – you'll have a great time. The sea, the sun, plenty of time to practice your speeches, right? And you get to see Athens! I would have killed to see Athens when I was your age!"

I asked if he wasn't forgetting that Caesar would be extremely grateful.

"Don't joke," Gaius said gravely. "I'm offering you the chance of a lifetime. In the heart of civilization. All expenses are on us. Besides," he added, with true sincerity, "look at it this way: would you prefer to go on holiday, or would you prefer to stay here and get tricked into more bread-delivering?"

When he put it like that, I knew I couldn't refuse. I was Caesar's man, trusty and true, and I was going to get away from Rome, from Caesar, from Gaius, and from Paulla as quickly as could be.

The Stowaway

For once, Gaius was as good as his word. I was equipped with every luxury. They packed my traveling trunk full of good clothes, my cloak, a dagger, and even the little packets of dried fruit and berries that were my favorite. Best of all, I had the collected speeches of the great Roman statesmen, on beautiful scrolls with silver handles, in polished oak cases. Gaius himself had gone down to the bookseller to buy them for me. Life could be worse, I reflected.

I wrote to my parents to say I would be traveling. They would be happy when they heard about my destination. Only a few young men, as a rule, got to see Athens and study in the great schools of philosophy and oratory there – such things were very expensive. My parents would be overjoyed that I was going there so young, and that Gaius was paying. I left out the spying.

The only downside was that I was traveling alone, with no servant. At such short notice, and at that time of year, Gaius's gang could find just one ship bound for Athens, and the only cabin available was too small for two people. Gaius gave me the letter of introduction to the ship's captain, along with thirty gold pieces. The cabin would cost ten, he said, and the rest was mine for Athens. I put them safe in the wallet I kept in my toga pouch.

Last of all, he gave me a sealed letter of secret instructions.

"Open it when you reach Athens," he told me. "It gives the name of our agent over there, and proof that you've been sent by me. He'll help you."

I was traveling mostly by ship, instead of taking the usual route by land to Brundisium and across from there to Greece; it was slower, Gaius said, but it was also the route which Spurinna was taking on his trireme warship. Moreover, Gaius was sure I would be followed and spied upon if I went by land. "This way you're safe on the wide blue sea and that's that," he said. We shook hands at the door.

With the trunk packed up on a mule cart and myself on horseback, it took most of the day to reach Ostia, the port of Rome, on the coast. The road ran down through the empty winter fields beneath gray clouds, and I cursed Spurinna (not for the last time) for choosing to sail in that dangerous season.

I had only been to Ostia once, but it was hard to get lost. The road led straight to the grand harbor. There was not much shipping in the port, apart from the navy warships, and even those were mostly pulled up on the beach in case of storm. I looked for the vessel Spurinna was on – Gaius had said it was called the *Rapacious*, with a red-and-white checked prow – but there was no sign of it. It was doubtless far down the coast already.

"Which one is mine?" I asked the mule driver – none other than the scrawny fellow who had pushed the bread cart behind me the previous summer. I surveyed the triremes with some satisfaction. They were tall masted, long, and sleek. Three banks of oars lay slack at their sides, glinting in the evening sun. I couldn't wait to see the inside of one.

"Well, sir, I'm afraid it's none of those, sir," said the mule driver. Instead, he pointed behind me to what looked like an enormous barrel tied up at the wharf. "That's it there, the *Star of Carthage*."

"That thing?" I cried. "That's not a ship!"

It was indeed a ship, however: a merchantman, and as unlike the tall triremes as you could imagine. Its bow was not reminiscent of a ferocious eagle's beak, and nothing about it was gleaming. The prow looped up in a long semi-circle ending in a statue of a goddess, but the waist of the ship was wide; at the stern it dropped abruptly down to the water. Worst of all, there were no oars: instead it relied on a vast lateen sail, slung at a steep angle from the single mast. Still, it was floating, albeit not very high in the water: it was deeply laden, nearly ready to depart. Four sailors were lifting the last of the cargo into the hold, swinging it from wharf to ship by means of a creaky crane.

Seeing me, two of the sailors came up and lifted my trunk onto the wharf, and the Captain approached.

"You're here," he commented.

"I'm here," I confirmed.

The Captain was a man of few words. He was short and a bit hefty. He had a thick black beard, huge forearms, and more than one tattoo. Apparently he and his crew were from Carthage. Nevertheless, something in his quiet manner inspired confidence. I handed over the letter of introduction and the ten gold pieces. He counted them silently.

"Welcome," he said.

I walked up the narrow gangplank, leaving the sailors to carry up my trunk. The first mate was cursing at them to get a move on: the evening breeze wouldn't wait. The deck was indeed as broad as I had imagined, tapering to the bow; it smelled of salt and paint. The vessel looked better up close. A door led to the cabin at the stern, lovingly painted with an image of Baal, the Carthaginian god. As I looked, a man emerged from behind it.

"You must be my fellow passenger!" he remarked, bowing, with a glance at my toga. He was wearing one himself, though it was rather too large for him; in one hand he was holding a pen, absentmindedly, as though he had lost the papyrus he was writing on and had resolved not to lose the pen as well. He was about thirty-five, and spoke with a Greek accent. I decided he must be a freedman, a former slave.

"That's me," I said.

"I think you will find your cabin on the left, sir," the Greek added, with another bow, and went to speak with the Captain. He was right. I opened the door and found the little room I would inhabit during the voyage. It featured a desk, a chair, and a hammock strung across from wall to wall. There was a small cupboard as well, and a fine spot for my trunk. Walls and floor were spotlessly clean.

I lay down in the hammock and thought, *Marcus, here the journey begins*. The ship was rocking slightly, even at anchor. From the small cabin window I could hear the sailors heaving and the Captain giving orders.

I went back up on deck. The sun was falling to the horizon and the light was failing; the end of the wharf was almost dark. I saw that my trunk was still sitting there in the shadows.

"Hallo there," I called to the first mate. "Haven't you got my trunk on board yet?"

"Not yet, sir," he answered with a sigh. "All this cargo! But we'll see to it right away, sir, we will." And he went with a man to bring it up.

They hauled it with difficulty to the gangplank.

"What have you brought, sir?" the first mate joked. "Going to build a house of bricks in Greece?"

Skillfully, they lifted it with the crane onto the deck, adding the last of the cargo. Then at a word from the Captain all four of them set to pulling up the anchor. After that, two men drew in the gangplank while the others climbed the mast and let fall the sail. The inshore breeze of dusk was still blowing and the sail filled quickly. Soon the wharf and the breakwater of the harbor were left behind. We were on the open Mediterranean, and a silver moon was rising. The Captain cleared his throat to show his satisfaction.

"A good breeze," he remarked. "We'll take advantage."

The wind held up, and the ship proved surprisingly swift, riding the light swells like a seabird afloat. The coast of Italy was lost in darkness.

I had just decided to go below and try sleeping when there came a dull thud.

"Eh?" grunted the Captain with surprise.

The peculiar noise was repeated. I wondered if the ship was going to buckle from the weight of cargo. This was a real thumping, however, and of all places it seemed to be coming from my trunk, which still lay on deck.

The Captain gave me a frown and went to open it. He lifted the latch and the lid flew open. Someone took a great gulp of air. A man was inside! The Captain hauled him out in an iron grip.

"Please!" the man squealed. "Don't throw me overboard!"

But the Captain was a gentle soul. He put the stowaway down at once, and the man sat there as the Greek passenger and the crew ran up. The man had bright, blond hair: a northern barbarian. The crew was not happy.

"You're a stowaway!" shouted the first mate, with a curse.

"I'm not!" the man cried, in a high-pitched voice. "Well, I guess I am. I mean, I was in the trunk, I admit that. But you must take me to Athens! It's – it's a matter of love!"

This was puzzling to them. Love did not feature prominently in a Carthaginian merchant's life.

"What?" the Captain inquired.

"My true love is going to Athens," was the explanation, "and I must follow or I must perish!"

"I vote for perish!" said the first mate fiercely.

"Certainly not," said the Captain sharply. "No. But you can't follow in this ship." He tugged at his beard. "You'll go ashore. At the next port. We can't turn back, with the breeze," he ended, as though he were sorry to report the fact.

"No!" the man yelped. "No, I must go on! All right, if you want to know the truth . . ."

Here the stowaway grabbed the back of his own head, seized hold of his hair, ripped it off, and tossed it to the deck. The crew leaped back in terror.

The Captain was made of sterner stuff. "A wig!" he exclaimed.

So it was. In place of the short, blond hair there now fell black ringlets, expertly coiffed. The stowaway stood up and curtsied prettily.

"Paulla!" I shrieked. With the disguise gone, Paulla had appeared on deck, as if by magic.

She spun toward me and did a triple-take. "Marcus!" she shrieked. "You!"

The Captain frowned at me. "You know this girl?"

I was stunned. I could not speak.

But Paulla, to be fair, was quick. "Here he is!" she cried, running up to me. "Marcus Oppius, my husband!" She kissed me on both cheeks.

"Your husband?" cried the Captain, amazed.

"My own true love! We're going to Athens." She dug her elbow into my ribs in a gesture of affection.

"Er, yes, that's right," I said, gulping. This was a nightmare.

The crew stared at me and then drifted off grumbling. The Greek passenger observed that we could certainly not throw her overboard now.

"You Romans certainly have strange ideas about how to transport your wives," growled the Captain; but then he grinned. "Did you think you could keep her hidden all the way to Greece?"

I felt dizzy. "I'll pay an extra ten gold pieces," I promised. It didn't seem like the right moment to correct him about me and Paulla.

The Captain stroked his great beard, considering. "Yes," he said simply, and went to take the steering oar. Paulla darted below – to *my* cabin. The Greek passenger and I were left alone.

"That was very nice of you, sir," he commented.

"What do you mean?" I demanded.

He grinned. "I mean this business, sir. As a student of the Muses, I am well versed in the complications of the human heart. In the words of the poet:

But with her hands the woman ope'd the jar,
Seal broken, scatt'ring troubles wide and far.

Very apt, don't you think?"

"Look," I said. "Who are you?"

"I am a publisher," the Greek said proudly. "I am going to Athens with this manuscript." He indicated a sheaf of papyrus sheets under his arm. The pen had gone missing. "My name is Aulus Lucinus Homerus. You can call me Homer, sir, though I am a Roman citizen."

"Marcus Oppius," I said, shaking his hand and trembling slightly all over. "Did you really just say your name was Aulus Lucinus Homerus?"

"Indeed I did, sir," said Homer. "I received that name when my master gave me my freedom. His name was . . ."

"Don't tell me. Aulus Lucinus Spurinna. The hero."

"Why, yes," Homer answered, surprised. "I was his secretary during the recent events, and I confess I played a slight role in them. But I can see you are a man of intellect, sir, like myself. To quote Hesiod once more, if I may:

Upon the twentieth morn a wise man's born

I would guess, sir, that you were born upon the twentieth morn?"

"What? What are you talking about?"

"I only mean that you showed wisdom in your dealings tonight, sir. The young lady may not be married to you, but I am glad she is on board and not overboard."

"I – well, how did you guess that?" I began. But at that moment Paulla reappeared from below. Somehow she had found a simple dress – I suppose she had brought it with her – and she was running my comb through her hair.

I tried to keep an even temper. She lounged against the rail and laughed.

"Are you crazy?" I demanded. "No, forgive me – you *are* crazy!"

"It's a long story, Marcus," she replied, regarding Homer with interest.

"It's getting longer every minute!" I cried.

"I'm going after Aulus," she said. "I have to. The heroines always do that."

"Heroines? What heroines? This isn't a novel!"

Paulla sighed. "It's because you've never been in love, Marcus. You've never even read about it. Those scrolls you had – they were more of those boring speeches, weren't they?"

I stared at her. "What do you mean, *had*?" I demanded. "And how on earth did you end up on this boat? Does your family know?"

"Ah, that's just it, Marcus. I've run away! I've escaped!"

I goggled at her, and she laughed again. Roman girls simply didn't run away: it was unthinkable, especially when your clan was the Aemilii.

"You're joking," I said. "Tell me you're joking!"

"It wasn't easy, let me tell you," she went on, ignoring me completely. "My father stationed guards outside my door! They knew I was upset about Aulus, you see, and they thought I might try something desperate. So I had to be clever. But that very night I was reading *The Sagacious Princess* and there it was, in the sixth chapter! The girl asks for a cup of wine before bed, and she only drinks a little and puts it outside the door with the guard. But first she puts a sleeping potion in the wine, and the guards fall asleep. Isn't that clever?"

I was still too appalled to speak.

"Where did you get the sleeping potion?" asked Homer.

"I didn't have one, so I just ordered more wine. They got drunk on it and they dozed off. I put on my disguise – I got that idea from *The Sicilian Story*, I'm sure you remember it – and pretended I was a slave going to buy firewood. Then I walked down to Ostia – it took all day – and I waited for a ship to Athens."

"But how did you know which ship to take?" I demanded.

"Really, Marcus, I just asked. There aren't many at this time of year."

"And my trunk?"

"I didn't know it was your trunk. It was just sitting there in the dark. Anyway, I wasn't going to stow away in a jug of honey. I'm sorry about your things, but there just wasn't any room. You certainly don't pack light."

"My things?"

"All those boring speeches, and that knife, and those clothes you didn't need. I did save one package of fruit, but it looked so delicious that I . . ."

I rushed to the trunk. Sure enough, it was as light as a feather, now that Paulla was no longer inside.

"My scrolls! My speeches! The secret instructions! It's empty!"

"Don't worry, Marcus," she replied soothingly. "You would have got bored with them anyway. I brought some novels with me instead. Quite a few of them, actually."

"They're unreadable," I moaned.

"Excuse me, sir," broke in Homer. "But, as a publisher, doubtless I can help. I have a delightful book with me, the one I'm taking to Athens. Just the thing for a young man like you, sir." He produced the first papyrus sheet from under his arm.

Gratefully, I took it down to my cabin and lit a candle. The first line said it all.

Aulus, there is no question of your going to Rome. You have not finished your studies, it read.

With that, I collapsed. I was trapped on a long voyage with Paulla and a crazy Greek, and all I had to read were the heroic adventures of Aulus Lucinus Spurinna.

The African Wind

And so our cruise along the coast began. At first we made excellent progress. The *Star of Carthage* was suited to the light northern breeze which filled the huge sail. For seven days it plowed steadily through calm seas, with the dolphins jumping before the bow. The winter days were short, but this pleased the Captain, who preferred to navigate by the stars. The mornings dawned cool and clear. To the east, the cliffs of Cumae and the islands of Ischia and Capreae slid past us. At noon one day, the Captain pointed out the lofty peak of Mount Vesuvius. Its steep slopes, furrowed with vineyards, bespoke the benefits of Roman peace.

In fact, the fine weather was surprising. Since the days of the ancients, sailors have dreaded the African Wind in winter, which blows from the southwest and drives ships against the rocky coasts, but so far there was no sign of it. The crew began each day with a song to Baal, to thank him for that fact, while the Captain kept one fist on the steering oar and beat time with the other. Homer suggested various other Winds they could sing to, complete with their extensive mythological characteristics; but they merely smiled and thanked him for his interest.

All in all, it would have been wonderful, if I hadn't been bored stiff.

The *Star of Carthage* was not a roomy ship. Apart from the Captain's cabin, and Homer's, and the crew's tight quarters, and the open deck, there was only the space I was now forced to share with Paulla. She and I agreed that we would each get eight hours in the hammock for sleeping and then divide the remaining eight hours between us. Still, it was cramped. Apart from a dozen scrolls (each containing a Greek romance novel), Paulla had also managed to bring four or five dresses, which she draped on every available surface. She had tossed most of my clothes into the harbor at Ostia.

So we all saw a lot of each other. The Greek publisher and I, in particular, spent a lot of time at the prow, looking at the dolphins. He liked to recite as many poems about them as he could remember, sometimes more than once. Everything seemed to remind him of a quotation, though he returned most often to his favorite, the poet Hesiod.

"Another fine day!" Homer would begin, joining me and looking at the beautiful coast. "I mean:

Indeed they dwell, untouched by woe or grief
On Blessèd Isles by swirling Ocean's reef.

Wouldn't you agree, sir?"

By which he meant, "Quite the view, isn't it?"

"If you say so," I replied. "How exactly did a freedman like yourself learn all this poetry?"

"Well, as a publisher," he began, "it is my profession to select the very best and, as you may have noticed, the very best is often to be found in Hesiod. But before I was the secretary of Lucinus Spurinna, I used to be a slave in Athens. It was my job to look up all the learned allusions made by my Athenian master's intellectual enemies, so naturally I picked up a lot, as you might say."

"Were they often wrong?"

"Usually. I would instruct my master in the correct allusions, so that he could humiliate his enemies the next time he saw them."

"Are you from Athens?"

"No indeed," Homer answered with a smile, "though I grew up there, sir, in a manner of speaking. I was born on the small island of Tragias, in the Dodecanese. But when I was ten years old, the island was attacked by pirates, who kidnapped me and sold me as a slave. I have always been very attached to Tragias, though I have never been back there, and I am afraid it is not mentioned by any poets."

"None?"

"No, none," Homer said sadly. "I feel that Hesiod *would* have mentioned it, if he had lived longer. Perhaps he *did* mention it, and the enemies of Tragias removed those lines from our collection of his verses. The excellence of its pears must have been proverbial, even in his time. It still is, on Tragias."

"Then why are you going back to Athens?"

He was going back, it transpired, because of the manuscript he had shown me – Spurinna's memoirs. It was too expensive to pay copyists to write out new copies of the book in the City, Homer said, or at least too expensive for the wide circulation that Homer had in mind. He would get the copying done in Athens, he thought. Maybe he would even buy some good copyist slaves there and bring them back to Rome.

"Have you finished reading it, sir?" he inquired. "I noticed it lying in the hammock in your cabin."

As a matter of fact, I was rather enjoying the story. It was remarkable how many clever things Homer had done, as Spurinna's secretary, in helping to stop Catiline's conspiracy. No doubt that was why Homer was publishing the book. Spurinna himself was less insufferable than I had expected: rather naive, of course, but he always meant well. In fact, if it hadn't been for Paulla's constant crooning over the absent young man, I might have taken to the fellow.

"We are separated as only star-crossed lovers can be!" she exclaimed one evening, as we ate our ship's biscuits together in the cramped cabin.

"You're not lovers," I pointed out. "There's only one lover involved here."

"But I *am* star-crossed," she insisted. "I have to share a cabin with you, don't I?"

"*I'm* the one who's star-crossed," I corrected her. "Your clan probably thinks you ran off with me, and they'll want to murder me!"

She smiled indulgently. "They may be very upset, Marcus, but they're not crazy: what girl would do that?" Then she sighed again. "Where do you think Aulus is right now? Do you think he is on his warship, slicing through the purple-crested sea?"

I thought of Spurinna's swift trireme, already countless miles ahead of the slow-moving *Star of Carthage*.

"Well, it's still February," I mused, "so he can't have saved Admiral Pompey's life more than once yet. But then again, he's probably met some nice Greek girl by now and –"

"Oh, Marcus, you're impossible!" she yelped, biting into her biscuit.

Here I made a serious mistake. I suppose I felt bad about teasing her, so I offered her a trade: she could read the Spurinna memoirs if she lent me her Greek novels. It was only adding fuel to the fire, of course, but I was desperate for something to do. A ship can be a tiny place.

Thus, as we rounded the toe of Italy and began our trip across the Ionian Sea to Greece, I started on *The Sicilian Story*. To my surprise, I found it quite original. The gallant young hero is forced to leave his homeland of Syracuse on the day before he is supposed to marry a princess, but he gets shipwrecked on a barren shore and then enslaved by an evil landowner. Meanwhile, the princess – our heroine – pretends to kill herself from grief at the departure of the hero. Helped by a fatherly ship's captain, she sails in pursuit of our hero and, unfortunately, gets captured by pirates. The Pirate King takes pity on her, however, and she disguises herself as the evil landowner's uncle and escapes. The Pirate King vows to destroy our hero's homeland in revenge, but after a terrific battle the hero saves the city of Syracuse and marries the heroine. Quite satisfying, I decided.

The next one I borrowed was *Hippias and Melite*. In this one, when the heroine, Melite, is traveling to Rhodes to marry the gallant young hero Hippias, she unfortunately gets shipwrecked on the barren shore of Egypt, where she is captured by bandits. Hippias, however, disguises himself as a Pirate King (who also happens to be the bandit chieftain's uncle), and travels in pursuit of the bandits. Using a sleeping potion, the heroine tries to escape from the bandit chieftain, but unfortunately the hero (still in disguise) drinks the potion by accident. The bandit chieftain is unfortunately captured by pirates, however, and attempts to kill himself from grief when he cannot understand how his uncle can be in two places at the same time. They all end up on a ship together, and after the most unfortunate shipwreck they travel to Rhodes where Hippias and Melite get married. In the end, the bandit chieftain takes pity on his uncle and everyone lives happily ever after.

In the third novel, *The Romance of the Happy Strangers*, the hero, traveling to Alexandria, is unfortunately shipwrecked on a barren shore in Thrace, where he becomes a shepherd. (Here I sat up, expecting some gripping realism.) The heroine, however, hoping the hero has not killed himself from grief, hires a fatherly ship's captain to go in search of him. After they are captured by pirates, however, it turns out that he is actually the uncle of the Pirate King, who is himself a landowner in Thrace. Disguising themselves as sheep, the Pirate King, heroine, and fatherly ship's captain give the hero (who is their shepherd) a sleeping potion. He discovers it in time, however, and takes pity on them, and in the end the hero and heroine sail to Alexandria to get married.

In the fourth one . . . but my mind was beginning to blur. By the time I finished the fifth novel, the world around me – the *Star of Carthage* on its slow, steady course, the voice of Homer quoting poets at the prow – seemed more and more like a Greek romance. After the sixth, I asked the first mate directly if he had ever been a bandit chieftain. After the ninth, I even grabbed Homer by the hair one afternoon and shouted, "You're a shepherd in disguise, admit it!" before they ushered me down to the cabin with a cup of hot wine.

After that, in the last part of our journey, I gave up reading and spent more time with the Captain. He was, as I said, a man of few words, and *romance* was not in his limited vocabulary. He had steered us flawlessly so far; but of course he came from a long line of merchants. His great-great-grandfather had been a captain in the Carthaginian navy, when they battled the Roman fleet in the Punic Wars. Now the family was less glorious but more prosperous. His sons, he said, would make fine ship captains.

"How old are they?"

"Twelve, ten, nine, seven, five, and two," he answered proudly. "But the two year old will make the best sailor of them all. You should see him with his toy boat in the bath!" Here, the Captain, who was also a man of few laughs, chortled heartily and stroked his great black beard. He couldn't wait for his sons to get tattooed. He told me of his house in Carthage, and his dear wife, and of the large statues of Baal and Tanit (Baal's wife) that they had helped build in the great temple there.

"Baal is the same as the one you Romans call Saturn, the father of Jupiter," he explained. "You know, of course, that the first human beings '*lived in those days when Saturn reigned supreme*,' as Hesiod says."

I looked at the Captain with concern. Obviously, during our voyage, someone had been having a bad influence on him. I changed the subject at once.

"How long will it take us to reach Athens?"

"From here?" he said. "Well, that is the headland of Messenia that you see there, off the port bow. Soon we will round the coast of Laconia, and from there it is three days sailing to Athens. Of course, much depends on the wind. Here, my Roman friend, why don't you take the steering oar for a while and tell me of your family?"

That night the storm hit us.

I was asleep in my hammock when I felt the ship's motion change. Usually it was a gentle sway, like the rocking of a cradle, and quite pleasant when you got used to it; but this was different, a violent lurching. I woke up to the sound of feet stamping along the deck and the first mate shouting orders. Paulla stuck her head past the cabin door.

"Sleeping again, Marcus?" she called. "Come out, you won't want to miss this!"

Grumbling, I followed her out and found all hands heaving to shorten the sail; the Captain was roping the steering oar in place. The air was much warmer than it had been. At the rail, Homer and Paulla were staring at the southern sky. I saw why. Great piles of red cloud had gathered there, and even as we watched they seemed to be flowing across the sunset toward us. The Captain looked at us and shook his head.

"It is the African Wind," he said.

Hour by hour, the breeze grew more intense. The sea turned dark blue and split into larger and larger swells. At sundown, a sprinkling of dust came falling from the red clouds: it was sand, carried by the wind from the distant desert of Libya.

"By Pollux," muttered Homer, subdued for once. "This will be a night indeed –

Now keep no ships upon the wine-dark sea
But surely stick to land, as I decree."

"More like the dark black sea," I commented, glancing at the rising hills of water that encircled us. The *Star of Carthage* was no longer sailing through them. Rather, we felt that the ocean's hand was raising us up on their backs and then lowering us into their depths. Every swell seemed taller and deeper than the last.

Paulla was quite calm. "Sailing in winter, what do you expect? Don't panic, Marcus, you've seen the Captain: he won't drown in a hurry."

If the Captain would not, I wasn't sure about the rest of us. With the sun gone, the enveloping night was utterly starless. The wind howled through the rigging and the ship

lurched ever more violently. Crew and captain labored
without rest: it took three of them to shift the steering oar,
pointing the *Star of Carthage* into the wind so that no wave
could strike us in the rear and smash the stern. Spray swept
the length of the deck, drenching us all. We three passengers went below. I lay sprawled on the floor, feeling terribly ill. From across the corridor we overheard poor Homer
being sick. Paulla lay in the hammock, reading by the light
of a single swaying lamp attached to the deckhead above.

All night there was no end to the fury of the storm. If I
had thought the wind intense before, it now revealed its
true power. The creak of ship's timbers was deafening, and
the first mate's voice, screaming orders through the gale,
was the only human sound on that tormented stretch of
sea. At length, we heard another: a rough music of voices.
It was the crew singing to Baal, passionately begging the
god to spare us. That was more terrifying than the storm
itself. Homer rushed on deck to join them.

Then the mast broke. We heard the horrible sound of
wood ripping, and the ship heaved over, nearly capsizing.
The crew took axes and hacked it free from the hull, and
we righted. But now, without her mast and sail, the ship
was a helpless toy for the waves and the implacable wind.

"The land! By Baal, the land!" came a scream from the
deck.

I could stand it no longer. I rushed out into the night
once more. My eyes beheld a nightmare scene: before us

loomed a blackness deeper than the sky, and the ship was being driven straight toward it; the sailors were calling aloud to each other and to heaven, in voices high pitched with terror; Homer was stuffing his manuscript into a watertight oilskin bladder; and, where the steering oar had been, the Captain was standing like a statue, glowering at the approaching headland as though defying the rocks to grind him and his ship to bits.

"Hold fast!" he cried at last.

A moment later we struck. Or rather, we sheered off one rock and bounced against another. There was a tremendous *boom* and the ship spun round, perpendicular to the swells. It rose on one last wave and seemed to be lifted across a battlement of rocks. Then it plunged and flew to pieces.

Everything rose into the air and you could no longer tell up from down. I was tossed into the seething sea. Suction drew me deep down and my ears felt like they would burst. Then I was up again, as if by magic, and I struggled frantically for air: I knew I must be sucked down again. My forearm smashed against something – a piece of wood – before I went under. My toga was like lead, and I kicked it off. This time I swallowed water and my lungs seemed to explode. As I came up, I flailed again, and again I felt the wood. I grabbed hold with both arms.

"Marcus!"

It was Paulla's voice, as though from a long way off.

"Marcus, you idiot!"

A wave submerged me, but I held fast. A feeling of horror crushed me. How had I left her below in the cabin? Now she was dead! It must be her spirit crying out to me, castigating me, as it fled from a watery grave.

"Marcus! Make room, by Juno!"

A hand slapped my wrist. I looked to my right. There was Paulla – a very wet Paulla – clinging to my bit of timber.

"Get your own plank!"

"Paulla, I . . ."

Another wave engulfed us, though it receded more swiftly than the others. The wind was slackening.

"All right then, kick with your feet!" she shouted. "Come on now!"

With what strength I could muster, I kicked at the water behind me. Over and over again we were lifted high and then dropped, and still we kicked. At last, as we dropped once more, we landed, and I felt the timber bite into my chest. It was stuck on something. Paulla was pulling at my shirt, dragging me forward. I crawled. The waves still broke over us, while I dug my feet into the loose rocks, inch by inch. At last there were no more waves, and she collapsed beside me. And, by Hercules, she laughed.

"We're alive!" she yelled.

"Alive!" I whispered as I shut my eyes. But then I remember nothing more.

5

The Barren Shore

I was roused by the crying of seagulls. My body ached. I was lying on my side, dry, in the glittering sun.

"He's awake!" called a voice in Latin, with a slight Greek accent.

I blinked hard, and when I opened my eyes I saw Homer squinting down at me. He had lost his toga and his hairline was fringed with salt. He was using a bit of driftwood as a crutch.

"I'm coming! Don't let him get away, Homer!" Paulla called.

I sat up. She was jogging along the steep beach toward us. Homer gave me a hand up, but at once I doubled over, retching salt water.

"Still some of the wine-dark sea left in there, I see!" he exclaimed sympathetically.

"I'm glad to see you too, Homer," I mumbled, as he helped me to a nearby rock. There I sat gasping. But the life was returning slowly to my battered limbs.

"Marcus! You look bad," said Paulla, as she ran up. She brushed my sleeve. "Bruised, aren't you? And your shirt is ripped. No thread, I'm afraid. Not much of anything, for that matter."

She had tied her hair into a bun, and a bruise was darkening on her chin, but otherwise she looked just fine.

While I recovered, they filled me in. Homer, whose knee was badly twisted, had remained beside me; Paulla had begun to explore the area. From where we were sitting I could follow her description. We were on a narrow stretch of beach at the far end of a long, narrow bay. Behind us on every side rose steep cliffs. To our left stood a rocky promontory tipped with white, glaring in the sunlight. About halfway between, in the middle of the bay, there rose three jagged pillars of sea-worn stone: the *Star of Carthage*, she supposed, had ricocheted off the first two and then smashed on the third. It had been broken into a hundred pieces and then pummeled over and over again against the rocks.

Homer, it transpired, had jumped overboard just before the ship struck.

"It seemed the natural thing to do, sir," he said casually. "How was I to know a person could be hurled through the air from the deck of a ship, like you and the lady here, and then gently washed ashore?"

"'Gently' isn't how I would describe it," I replied. "But, Homer, it was sheer madness to try swimming in that sea!"

"I'm afraid, sir, that I cannot swim. Instead, as a

publisher, I naturally relied upon my manuscript. I sewed it up, you see, in this bladder, which I inflated." He pointed with his driftwood crutch at the oiled bladder, evidently still containing Spurinna's memoirs, which lay in the shade of our rock. Beside it lay what Paulla had managed to collect from the wreckage strewn along the beach.

She had not found much. There was the plank Paulla and I had used for swimming – it turned out to be half of the main cabin door, featuring the left side of Baal's head. It made me think sadly of the Captain and his wife back in Carthage, so proud to contribute to the god's great statue. There were several ropes, their ends rubbed to threads: the remains of rigging. There was the handle of the steering oar. And last, but certainly weirdest, there was Paulla's blond barbarian wig, sopping wet and full of seaweed.

"Still wearable," she claimed. "It's high quality, Marcus. You get what you pay for." But she declined to try it on.

I looked at my companions. Were they in denial, giddy from having survived certain death? They seemed unnaturally talkative. Upon what barren shore had we been shipwrecked? Was this the end of my mission for Gaius? Most of all, I wondered, what on earth could we hope to do now?

But Paulla and Homer had already discussed this point.

"Now that you're better, Marcus," said Paulla firmly, "we must at least walk around the bay. Perhaps there are other survivors."

So, wearily, we began to walk the narrow beach, beyond the limit of Paulla's first explorations. We hoped to find some of the ship's cargo washed ashore, for at the moment we had nothing to eat or drink. Leaving Homer with our few possessions there on the beach – our "marching camp," as Homer called it with satisfaction – Paulla and I started toward the rocky promontory, stumbling along the loose stones, shells, and driftwood. The cliffs rose on our left; to our right was the peaceful horizon. To my dismay, we could see no sign of my toga (or the ten gold pieces which I kept in its pouch). It must have been at the bottom of the bay.

Our first discovery was not a happy one. Two of the crew lay mangled at the water's edge. They had perhaps tried to help each other in the sea, for their limbs were entangled. Baal had forsaken them.

Now we came to a little cove, unseen from a distance until we stumbled upon its mouth. It was filled with wooden planks: the water, swirling into it, sloshed the wreckage about. Much of the ship's hull must be there, we decided, and then our hopes soared: bobbing inside it all were three amphoras, the great jugs which had made up the bulk of the ship's cargo.

"I'll go," I announced, and with Paulla's warnings echoing in the air I waded into the shallow water. Nail-studded beams and splinters blocked my path, but I waited for the rush of the waves that filled the cove and slowly made progress when they receded. I grabbed the handles – two in one hand – and found it was easier going back: free of the wreckage, the jugs would naturally drift out to sea.

"These are the only ones I saw in there," I told Paulla. "The others must be gone, or at the bottom of the bay."

The seals were intact, however, and both of us rejoiced: for the time being, at least, we would not starve. We lifted them to a dry place and went on down the beach.

When we had nearly reached the rocky promontory, we found the Captain. Or rather, we saw a huge white shape that we thought must be a great flat rock. As we approached, however, the rock seemed to flutter and wave, and then there was no mistake: it was the ship's sail, with the Captain squatting beneath it. He had lost his shirt, his beard was askew, and he seemed to be half dead, but his eyes glittered as we ran up.

"You see, Marcus," Paulla cried happily, "I told you he wouldn't drown in a hurry!"

He was overjoyed to see us.

"I'm so happy that both you and your wife survived!" he said, shaking my hand. It didn't seem like the right moment to correct him about me and Paulla.

He had already found the bodies of the last two sailors, including the poor first mate; and he had supposed his passengers were dead too. Being buoyant, he had been tossed by the waves most of the night, fighting them with his great strength, and been borne down the coast. But at last he had struggled to shore, and there, in the morning, he had found the sail.

"A curse upon this headland," the Captain growled. "If we had rounded it, we would all have lived. But, you know, the mast . . ." He trailed off. "I thought they would meet their end upon the deep, someday," he sighed, meaning the crew. "Not here, piled like fish on the land."

We decided to rejoin Homer at his "marching camp." But we were obliged to wait all afternoon while the sail dried in the sun: wet, it was impossibly heavy. We folded it neatly and the Captain got underneath, Paulla holding up the front and I taking the rear. Then we stumbled back along the beach.

Homer, in turn, had been busy. He had collected dried leaves and brushwood for a fire and, using an ingenious philosophical technique he had learned in Rome from a friend, he had twisted strands of the rope around a stick and was using it to drill sparks from a piece of driftwood. Unfortunately, he was getting nowhere until the Captain arrived and took over. With joy we saw the sparks leap up as the wooden drill tore into the log and Homer's dry leaves caught them as they flew.

Paulla and I left them to it, heading back with a rope for the great jugs. Paulla had the good idea to tow them through the surf along the shore, which we did as the sun fell swiftly down the cloudless winter sky.

We found the Captain and the publisher warming their

hands beside a good fire. The Captain was staring at the half-portrait of Baal, vowing he would return, aye, to Carthage and get a new boat, somehow. Homer was just proposing himself as the new first mate, so the Captain was delighted to see us appear with the jugs.

"I hope you like olives!" he chuckled, looking them over.

For it was indeed olives that the three jugs contained: enormous amounts of them, packed in their own juice. The problem of hunger and the problem of thirst were thus solved at one blow, but we all felt rather permeated by the taste and smell of them as we lay down by the fire to sleep that night.

At dawn the next day, we set to work on the sail. While Homer, with his twisted knee, stood aside and commented upon the various geometric angles we were producing, we hoisted the thing into the semblance of a tent. Driftwood logs made for fine pillars, four on the corners and a great bleached tree, buried deep in the sand, at the center. In the end, all four of us could sit or lie down comfortably inside it. We put stones around the central pillar and transferred the fire to a pit in the middle, with a hole in the roof for the smoke to escape. At the end of the day, we were very pleased with ourselves. Homer had been hobbling along the beach looking for shellfish, and that night we cut our olive ration with three clams apiece, baked in the sand beside the fire.

With shelter and food taken care of, our next priority was to bury the dead. Only the Captain knew the proper

Carthaginian rituals, though these (as it transpired) were difficult to perform, since we had no bronze statues of chariots and no pine torches. We settled for piling stones on the graves. The Captain cried beside the first mate's tomb.

For the next few days we took it easy. Everyone ached, from our labor as much as from the storm. We had no idea where we were, apart from the Captain's assertion that it must be somewhere in Laconia. The stars told us we were looking south across the bay, but we knew nothing more than that. My mission for Gaius was, at best, badly delayed – Cicero and Pompey would form an alliance after all. Paulla, shipwrecked, was as far from her lover as ever. Of course, her family would be searching for her already, but why would they ever search here? Only Homer remained optimistic, and he discoursed at length on the excellent opportunity we now had to show our philosophical calm.

It was indeed calm. As though exhausted by their encounter with the African Wind, the seas lay placid, gently slapping the beach at all hours. The gulls cried to one another, but there was no other sign of living being.

It was Paulla, as you might expect, who took things in hand.

"We can't sit here forever," she complained. "We've eaten two jars of this stuff already, and what will we do when the third one's gone? If we can stand a third one," she added.

"We'll have to go inland," I said. "There must be a village or two nearby."

"Inland?" she asked. "Past those cliffs? We'd never get Homer over them, with his leg. You and I will do it," she finished, "first thing tomorrow."

So we set forth to explore. We filled Homer's oilskin bladder with enough olives for a day, and left him with the Captain. First we tried the cliffs behind us. No luck. They were nearly vertical and rose a hundred feet down the entire shoreline as far as we could see, as though the gods had broken off the crust of the land with their fingers, leaving only the jagged edge and the stony beach.

So we turned west, the opposite direction from the headland where we had found the Captain. Here the beach was much narrower and the going was difficult. Often the shoreline was pierced by deep bays, and one had a water-fall pouring down it to the sea. We tried climbing up beside it, but the rocks were slick with spray and we turned back. In the end we had to swim across that bay; neither of us was a strong swimmer and it was a good distance. On the far shore we had lunch.

"I can feel we're close," Paulla claimed. "It's like in *The Twice-Told Tale*, when the hero is trapped in the dungeon and he has to examine every stone before he can escape."

"Twice-told is right," I remarked.

"Don't be sour, Marcus. Just a few stones to go."

So we pressed on. And soon enough, as she predicted, we reached another bay, where the river, flowing down from the highland, had cut its way through the cliff. The stream was little more than a trickle at that season and we could climb up the watercourse itself. One time Paulla slipped, but I was behind her and kept her from tumbling. At last we felt the northern breeze on our faces. We had reached the top.

Open meadow stretched on every side, dotted with clumps of pinewood. The contrast with the scene on the narrow beach was astonishing. Mountains rose in the distant north-east, topped with cloud; to the north-west was rolling pasture, crossed by a thin brown line.

"A road! A road, Marcus!"

It seemed a long way away, and the sun was already beginning to sink from its zenith, so we contented ourselves with taking off our sandals and walking in the long grass. As I was putting my sandals on again, I heard Paulla shout.

"Over here! Over here! Oh, can you hear me? We're over here!"

She was running swiftly over the plain toward a black dot on a far slope. Shading my eyes, I saw that it was indeed a human shape, but even as she ran the figure disappeared into the grass.

"There was someone there!" she gasped, walking back. "I'm sure of it. Do you think he saw me? He must have heard me!"

"I don't know," I said. "With this wind blowing toward us, he might not have. And we would be as small to his eyes as he was to ours."

There was nothing to do but go back. We descended the watercourse, telling each other we were sure Homer could manage it, and swam back across the bay. It was dark by the time we saw the glow of the firelit tent on the familiar stretch of beach.

That night we celebrated with an extra helping of olives, washed down with the weakest olive juice we could extract. Our friends were overjoyed at our good news. In our minds we were already home – or rather I was home, Homer was rich, the Captain had a new ship, and Paulla was again on her way to see Spurinna. We stayed up late with a good blaze, and the Captain taught us to sing his old Phoenician sea shanties. We were just drifting off when the Captain whispered, "Do you hear that?"

No sooner had he said it than a distant horn sounded through the darkness. We leapt up and rushed out – into the very arms of our enemies.

The tent was ringed by twenty men. Some of them carried pitchforks and shovels, but most carried spears. They had snuck up to us in the dark. As we flew out of the tent they caught hold of us, and suddenly torches were lit, flaring in the darkness. The men were bearded and their clothes stained and dirty. Their hands held tight to our shirts. Paulla emerged last from the tent. She had thrust the blond wig on top of her hairbun.

None of the armed men spoke. From down the beach, a horse whinnied and we heard it trotting forward.

"So you've caught them! Well done, for once," growled the horseman in Greek, coming into the torchlight. "What is this camp they've got? Burn it to the ground!"

He leaped nimbly from his horse. I saw that his clean-shaven face wore a scowl, his thick brows furrowed. He had a red cloak, and around his neck he wore a horn tipped with gold.

"You are trespassing on the property of Brasidas of Sparta," he barked. "*My* property."

"We did not know!" I protested. "That is, we were ship-wrecked – our ship foundered in this bay."

"Quiet!" he shouted. "Shipwrecked, trespassing, it's the same thing to me! And the same thing for you, young rascal! What is this crew you've got here – a Greek, a Phoenician, a barbarian and – what are you?" he snarled at me.

None of the others said a word. I was not so cautious.

"I'm a Roman!" I hurled back at him. "A Roman citizen, for that matter, and you'd better watch yourself!"

Brasidas laughed.

"Well, that's a new one," he spat. "A Roman citizen, are you? And I'm the King of Persia! Tell me, young slave, do Roman citizens usually go about in rags, unwashed, like you? What presumption! I myself have not yet achieved the honor of citizenship, though I will, by Castor, indeed I will, you mark my words."

"I'm no slave!" I shouted. "How dare you suggest –"

He slashed me with his riding crop. I ducked and took it on my head. He struck me there again.

"Take them away!" he snarled to his men. "Put them on the morning shift tomorrow!"

We were pushed along amidst the press of armed men. They drove us far from the tent and put it to the torch. Looking over my shoulder, I caught a glimpse of it lifted high in the air by its own great flame. With that, the last remnant of the *Star of Carthage* was no more.

The Plantation

I will never forget that horrible rush through the dark. As yet we had no chains on our feet, but in the minds of the men who were pushing and driving us we had already become human cattle. The torchlight illuminated nothing but the shadowy rocks we were stumbling over and the grins of our captors.

We were taken, as best as I could judge in the dark, toward the headland and around its farther side. There, half a mile past the spot where we had found the Captain, was a narrow path that climbed the cliff. The malevolent Brasidas left us, riding farther down the beach. The men with spears forced us ahead, up the path in single file to the dark and windy highland. From the top, it was four more miles to our destination, but it felt like one continuous effort to stay on my feet and avoid being dragged or trampled in the wet grass.

Now and again I caught sight of my friends' faces. Paulla had one hand clamped to her head, trying desperately to keep her wig on. The Captain was bellowing fiercely, cursing the men in Phoenician, and gasping at the exertion: he was not used to land. Homer alone maintained his calm, though the steep path must have been pure agony to his knee. I noticed he was holding his belly, which seemed fatter than I could recall. He had somehow managed to stash the oilskin containing his precious manuscript inside his shirt.

At last, dizzy with weariness, we reached a compound on the plain. In the dark I could just make out it was surrounded by a stockade of wooden stakes. We passed through a muddy gate.

"Put them in the stables for tonight. After that, you'll have to find room," one of the men barked gruffly. They spoke Greek, but the accent was rustic and very nasal.

We were pushed toward a low building and tossed into an empty stall inside. The straw smelled of mules. The man with the gruff voice came in afterwards and roughly attached leg-irons to our right ankles; then he drew a thick chain through all four of them. He withdrew, leaving us alone at last; but we did no more than exchange a glance of despair. With the chain tying us together, we could not hope to escape.

"Better to sleep, I believe," was Homer's only comment, and he fell asleep at once. The others soon followed.

For myself, I couldn't get a wink. My mind was spinning furiously. I sat there staring at the blackness. By Hercules,

I had read enough about such things, thanks to Paulla, but the stunning reality was more than I could take in. Could this happen to a Roman citizen? Wouldn't there be some sort of consequences for Brasidas and his men? With a shudder I realized there could not be: a thousand miles of sea lay between us and Rome, between Brasidas and justice. In any case, how would anyone ever find out we were there? It would take months to discover we had sailed for Athens and never arrived. Gaius and Pompey and Caesar and Spurinna would mourn for us, maybe, and then get on with their lives.

I was still thinking such unsettling thoughts when the cocks crowed. From outside the stable came the noise of a farm waking up. Pigs were grunting, chickens scurrying, and then came an ominous clanking of chains.

The stable door was pushed open. A tall figure was silhouetted against the dim light.

"Get up! Get up!" it bawled hoarsely. "Dawn's your cue, got it? Get up and see if you can earn your evening bread!"

There was no breakfast. We shuffled out the door and found we were facing a wide open yard, deep in mud, ringed with shabby wooden buildings. Beyond these rose the wall of the stockade. In the corners of the yard, various farm animals were prowling. But what caught my eye were the seventy human beings in the middle.

They were chained together, as we were, in files of ten. All of them were men. They were generally short, stubby types, of all ages, some gray-headed and several as young as Paulla and myself. Many had brown or red hair; on most it was falling past their ears, slicked back with its own grease. Their clothes were no more than rags. Beside them stood a couple of men with spears.

"Right, listen everybody!" shouted the man with the gruff voice, who seemed to be the overseer. "These are your new friends. Say your names!"

This was directed at us. Homer, the Captain, and I gave ours; but Paulla said nothing.

"You there, the barbarian boy! What's wrong with you? Give your name!" growled the overseer, striding toward her.

Paulla stared at him with open eyes.

"Your name! Name! Don't you speak Greek? Latin? Well, you'll go by Barbo, then. Right, now, you disgusting lot, get over there on the back end. You, Master Roman Citizen, you can make sure Barbo does what you do, got that? Right!"

The overseer barked another order and two women rushed out from the shadows. With a key, they unfastened the chain that held the four of us together, and we walked heavily over to the back of the slave column. They drew up the chain that bound seven of the others together and ran it through our leg-irons. We were now part of a file ourselves.

"Now, move!" cried the overseer, and the first file headed through the gate. Each file followed in turn, some splitting off for special tasks but most going straight ahead toward the fields. We passed a pile of farm implements and a man handed us each a shovel.

That first day, our file was assigned with two others to the barley fields. Since it was winter, these were empty of crops, but our job was to turn the soil to expose it to the air; if we found a rock we had to toss it into a pile behind us. I have always enjoyed hard work but, after an hour, I realized this was different. There was no stopping, for each file had a sub-overseer keeping watch with a whip. If a slave put down his shovel or even seemed too interested in the distant mountains of Laconia, the man was there with his blows and a shower of curses. The sun rose to its zenith, beating down on us. I longed for it to rain. My back and shoulders ached from the constant shoveling. I don't know how Paulla managed it.

At about the second hour they brought round some foul wine and some porridge, and we had a short break.

"Marcus, this is killing me!" muttered Paulla, with her head down. "Don't you feel the sun?" She was sagging.

I took a gulp of the foul wine. "You're right," I said. "But doesn't it remind you of *The Sicilian Story*, when the hero..."

That revived her. I learned quickly that, even though we were shipwrecked and enslaved, our plight was nothing like *The Sicilian Story*, though it did have some resemblance to *The Sad Spanish History*, given that Paulla was disguised as a barbarian.

"You'll have to help me sew this thing on tonight," she said, adjusting her wig. "I've been terrified the whole time it will fall off!"

"Why did you pretend you don't know Greek?" I asked.

"Because no one notices a barbarian. *Barbo* indeed!" she scoffed. "I'd like to teach that Chief Overseer what it means to insult the clan of the Aemilii!"

"Didn't you run away from the clan of the Aemilii?" I asked. "Anyway, now that you've pretended not to understand anything, you'll have to ignore everything he says. Don't react. Don't say anything if you can help it."

"I'll try, Marcus," she said gloomily.

From there the days ground on. Every day was like the one before. We had nothing to look forward to. We slept in stalls hardly better than the stables. It was the same straw, stinking of people and not of mules. Homer buried his oilskin deep inside it. After the first night, we weren't shackled while we slept or while we ate our small meal of bread and cabbage in the evening, talking with our fellow slaves in the guarded stall building. Paulla would usually slip off by herself then. Generally she had a hard time of it, since she was naturally so talkative, but she kept silent, except when we were alone. She was right about being ignored, though the other slaves were generally uninterested in us. There was a glassy look in their eyes. Many of them spoke no Greek, and none spoke Latin. They were about evenly divided between those who had been born in slavery – these were the more talkative ones – and those who had been captured in the wars. These last were mostly Thracians and Dacians, but some were from farther east, from Bithynia and Galatia.

"Sure, I'll tell you, boy," one of them finally said one evening: he was a tall man, awfully thin, with a scar down his cheek. "If you're so curious. I'm with my dad on the farm, see, and they put us in the army. King Mithridates, that was his name, but they never gave us a weapon. We walk up and down, up and down, and then my dad was killed in the big fight. And they take me, see, and put me on the ship, and then I get off that and the next thing you know I'm here. Ten years, I've been here. Ten years of this awful stuff."

"Did you ever try to get away?" I asked.

"Get away?" he sneered. "Ah, sure, there was the time I grew wings, wasn't there, when I flew over the mountains! When I grew scales and I swam the sea! That's right, boy, I'm only here by choice. I want to help, you see. Help the master with his barley and his olive trees."

"Shut up," said another slave. "None of that or we'll all be punished."

"You shut up, you pig," muttered the thin man, but he would say no more after that.

Such were our companions on the plantation. In their view, there could be no escape – the very idea barely registered. They were too busy, and they were always tired. We grew like them. The weeks flowed past, and I began to think that life in Reate hadn't been so bad. We got the planting done, toiling through the spring rain with the overseers bawling for us to hurry. Then there were the olive groves to tend, and for six days we quarried stone for an extension to Brasidas' villa. For ourselves, we concentrated on survival. My muscles grew thick, and even Paulla began to look more like the barbarian she claimed to be. We gave up all effort at keeping clean. The Captain's beard, which he refused to cut, even though the Chief Overseer screamed at him, grew long and incredibly bushy. He kept his faith that he would see Carthage again like a secret cache of gold in his mind. When we were alone he would talk of nothing but the sea.

For myself, I was the hardest worker in our file. The overseers seemed to have orders to single me out – they never forgot my absurd claim to be a Roman citizen – and the only way I could escape punishment was by never giving them an excuse. My friends followed my example, and we escaped the worst of it. But they flogged some of the Galatians. One of them had a hundred lashes for stealing food, and died soon after.

Brasidas himself we rarely saw. Occasionally he would ride through his fields, scowling, but mostly he kept to his villa. This, we learned, was down by the shore, but we never saw it, for we never left the highland or the stockade. They said he spent long evenings there, dictating to a horde of scribes and copyists. The universal opinion was that the house slaves at the villa had it easy. "Send him to the house" was the usual joke if one of us said something clever.

Homer, meanwhile, missed the planting season altogether. From the first, he had set himself to learning the local dialect and its nasal accent. To this end, he insisted on engaging our overseers in conversation. At first they rewarded him with blows, but before long the Chief Overseer would begin his morning inspection with a chat with Homer, standing in his file. They liked the fact that he talked like them. Indeed, after a while it was impossible to get him to speak normally: even his Latin became rustic and nasal.

"Homer," I told him, "this is getting ridiculous. You're not a yokel."

"No indeed, sir," he replied with a slight smile.

It was a month after our life on the plantation began, on an early April morning, when Brasidas happened to ride past us in the fields. Perhaps it was the sight of the first wildflowers in the fields, but he got off his horse close to where we working and turned to survey the rolling hills.

"My domain," he bellowed, holding his arms high. "The domain of a Spartan! When shall I return to you, Sparta? When shall I be restored to you?

O men of Heracles' unconquered race
Take heart, for Zeus has not yet turned his face!"

Terrific, I thought. *Just what we need: a cruel landowner who thinks great thoughts.*

Then another voice spoke, no less nasal than our master's:

"Dread not the press of men, and do not fear:
Let each his shield against the foeman steer
With ruthless spirit; dying's darksome fate
As welcome as the sunshine estimate."

All of us – slaves, overseer, and landowner – spun round to look at the man who had finished Brasidas's warlike quotation. It was, of course, Homer. For a moment we stood there frozen. It was unthinkable for a slave to address our master, and with precious little sign of deference at that. Then the overseer raised his whip.

"No talking!" he shouted, striding toward Homer's place in the file.

"No! On your life, do not strike him!"

Brasidas had grabbed the overseer's wrist.

"You'll strike when you're told to strike," he spat out fiercely. Then he turned to Homer, disbelief in his eyes. "Where on earth did you learn those verses, slave? Are you from Laconia?"

"Why, sir," answered Homer brightly, dropping his shovel. "I have always enjoyed that poem – the Spartan poet Tyrtaeus, is it not? Indeed yes," he said with satisfaction.

"Not quite as good as the true classic, however – how does it begin?

> *"I'll praise no man, nor his repute convey,*
> *Unless he's brave amid the bloody fray."*

Brasidas stood astonished for a moment. He seemed poised between laughter and deadly anger. At last he cleared his throat.

"'*Nor his repute* relay,'" he corrected. "But come now, answer my question. How is it that you know Tyrtaeus?"

"I have had occasion," said Homer judiciously, "to study that excellent poet, in my time. I have always regarded him as the Spartan Hesiod, if I may say so."

"Nonsense!" snorted Brasidas. "Tyrtaeus and Hesiod? Do you compare them? Tyrtaeus and that interminable old bore?" His anger welled once more.

Keeping stock still as I was, I mentally lifted my hands to heaven in prayer. *Please, Jupiter*, I prayed, *let Homer swallow the insult. Preserve him. Preserve us all.*

Homer stood for a moment considering. "You are right, sir," he said finally. "The remark was ill chosen. I only meant that Hesiod has done for the other Greeks what Tyrtaeus has done for Sparta."

"Right!" cried Brasidas. "And look at them! That's what happens," he went on, "from listening to those empty, blathering verses. Just what I've always thought. Come now," he said, gesturing to the overseer to release Homer from the chain, "were you a poet? A rhapsode? A singer?"

"Hardly that, sir," said Homer with dignity. "I was, as indeed I still am, a publisher."

"A publisher!" cried the landowner. "Do you mean, with copyists and manuscripts and all that? Circulating books? In Athens?"

"Certainly not, sir. In Rome."

"Rome!" Brasidas exclaimed. "But how did you come here?" His eyes strayed to the horizon. "In Rome, by Castor!" He bit his lip in thought. "Then you could do it, you, my slave, perhaps – perhaps . . ."

"Do what exactly, sir?"

But by that time they had passed beyond our hearing, strolling together back toward the stockade, the tall Spartan with his hands clasped behind his back and Homer gesturing amiably.

Paulla was looking at me in disbelief, the shovel poised in her hand.

"We're doomed," I whispered.

Thus Homer's ascendancy began. He was moved to the villa the next morning, pausing only to reclaim the oilskin from his pile of straw. We saw no more of him that spring. Yet we heard news of him from those slaves whose duties took them to the villa every so often, such as the woman who tended the pigs and sometimes led one down to the shore for slaughter.

"Your Greek friend's quite the darling these days, boy," she commented one afternoon. "He's always in with the master and those scrolls of his. Reading to him, I hear."

But before long they were no longer calling him "your Greek friend" or even "that wretched Athenian."

"New secretary's a smooth man," I overheard the Chief Overseer say to one of his men one day. "Promised to write me an overnight pass to the village if I sent him down some olive oil. Yes, write, like with a pen."

"But he was just in there with the gangs last month!" protested his companion.

"Never you mind about that," answered the Chief Overseer. "He's not someone you want to cross. If he hears you talking like that, he'll tell the master you killed his deer, or who knows what."

But soon even the Chief Overseer joined in the darker mutterings.

"Our master's bewitched," he told the guard at the slaves' quarters half a month later. "Who's he to go choosing that Estate Manager as his new heir, when he's got three sons already! And that fellow won't remember us kindly," he added. "Not when he was there in the fields with the rest of them."

As I reported all this to Paulla and the Captain, our hopes rose to ever greater heights. But somehow we never got the longed-for reassignment to the villa and its dreamed-of luxuries. We toiled on, and the moon waxed and waned, and summer was coming in, and the second month of toil was coming to an end, and still Homer sent no word. The overseers spared us the whip, for the most part, since it was known that Homer had been associated with us in the file, but even the Captain was getting worried.

"I hope our friend is still our friend," was his gloomy comment.

A third month went by, mostly spent planting. By now I had given up hope of ever seeing Reate and my parents again, much less fulfilling my mission for Caesar. There was barley to seed, and then an endless field of turnips. The days grew longer and longer, and we worked from dawn to dusk.

At last, one morning in late May, three months after the shipwreck, the guards were out in force for our dawn inspection, leaning on their spears. We stood in rows, as ever, but the command to start work never came; the overseer and the guards watched the sun rise higher.

"He's late!" he muttered. "Isn't that what you'd expect?"

Two hours later, a trumpet sounded and the door of the stockade swung in. Through the gate came four horsemen: a man in front, riding a white horse, and three scribes following.

Homer! I shouted inwardly, for there he was on that white horse, dressed in a splendid purple shirt, his hair cut short and an eagle feather in his hand.

"Chief Overseer!" he called as he dismounted. "I have come to take some of your slaves to the villa. I have detailed instructions," he said, waving a scroll at the illiterate brute. "Are they ready for inspection?"

"They are – sir," said the Chief Overseer through clenched teeth.

"Very good, very good. I see you are doing an excellent job overseeing," commented Homer as he walked down the line. "Now then, to business. I require one man with a large beard."

"Look for yourself, Estate Manager," replied the Chief Overseer. "The Carthaginian. As big a beard as you could ask. I didn't let him cut it, sir."

"Didn't you?" said Homer, with a severe look. "Yes, he's exactly right. Now then, what else?" He consulted his scroll. "Hmm, I need two young men. Do you have any slaves with blond hair?"

"Blond?"

"Exactly so. I require one to play a barbarian slave."

"Well," said the Chief Overseer with suspicion, "as you know, there's Barbo. But he doesn't talk."

"Which one is Barbo? It has been a while since I, er, since I visited the stockade."

Paulla stepped forward.

"Yes. Indeed, yes," said Homer. "A splendid fit. And that hair would make an excellent wig. Perhaps we can sell some of it afterwards. Now, lastly, we need someone for a Roman youth."

"If I may ask, Estate Manager, what exactly is all this for? We have the vines to prune today and I doubt if I can spare –"

"Quiet!" barked Homer. "That is, perhaps you might be more quiet, Chief Overseer. You are disturbing my concentration."

He strode down the files of slaves, giving the young men a good look. *By Hercules*, I thought, *pick me and get this outrageous act over with!*

"What about this fellow?" he said, stopping in front of me. "He's the one who claims he's a Roman citizen, isn't he? How absurd. Can you imagine such a person in a toga?"

I ground my teeth.

"I see you've put him to work," he continued. "Well done. Can't have the slaves getting delusions of grandeur, can we? Not with the planting season only just over! Dear me!"

I nearly reached out and took him by the neck. Homer had been living in the lap of luxury through that planting season.

"I suppose he'll do," he conceded at last, flicking me with his eagle feather regretfully. "But now, we must be off. The production is tonight, you know."

"The production? Production of what?" asked the Chief Overseer.

"The theatrical production, my good man," Homer replied with some condescension. "What exactly did you think I was talking about all this time? It is my latest improvement to the culture of this uncivil region. I myself will be starring in it. It is an adaptation, I am pleased to say, written by myself, of a famous historical account. The latest developments from Rome, dramatized for the tragic stage. It is called *The Conspiracy at Rome*. All the local people will be attending. There is considerable excitement, I may say, since even here" – he permitted himself a final sniff – "even in these remote and unwashed regions, they have heard of the exploits of Aulus Lucinus Spurinna."

7

The Tragic Stage

The door of the stockade shut behind us. We were suddenly in the open, and there were no chains on our legs. Counting Homer's horse and the three horses that the scribes were riding, we even had transportation. But Homer ordered the scribes to ride well behind us, out of earshot. Soon we had passed over a rise in the land and the dreadful plantation was lost to view.

"Well done, Homer!" I cried. "We can take the horses and ride for it!"

"Alas, sir, if only it were that simple," he answered with a sigh, abandoning (as I was pleased to hear) the nasal dialect. "Brasidas has several huntsmen and a pack of murderous hunting dogs. We would certainly be caught in the mountains. All this peninsula is his territory, and the only way off is by sea." He sounded sure of it. "But don't worry, sir, I have thought it through quite carefully."

"I'm sure you have," I said grimly. "It took you long enough. You've been living in luxury at the villa while we've been out plowing and shoveling!"

"I appreciate that, sir, but I assure you, I too have been laboring, and it has not been altogether pleasant."

"Oh, yes?" exclaimed Paulla. "And what exactly have you had to put up with, besides hot baths?"

"That madman's literary taste!" replied Homer vehemently. "Do you have any idea, madam, how horrible these Spartan poets are? By now I am familiar with every synonym for *carnage* and *combat* in Greek!" He began a long rant at this point, casting off three months of literary hypocrisy in one go.

"In any case," I interrupted, "it hasn't done you much harm. I could hardly keep up with all your titles. Surely it wasn't your charming personality?"

"No, sir. Well, not entirely. Brasidas, you see, has been exiled from Sparta. By the time he met me, he had already begun a very long work – incredibly long, sir, twenty-one full scrolls – entitled *The Vindication of Brasidas*. I have been helping him polish it, working day and night, adding endless niceties and ever longer quotations from Tyrtaeus. He yearns for a publisher, you see, and wishes me to circulate the finished *Vindication* back in Rome.

"My plan was working. I confess that I did have some part in extending his arguments; but I required more time and more influence if we were seriously to attempt to escape. All the while that bloodthirsty monster grew ever more dependent upon my literary taste. That is why he promoted me. I intended to use my new power to get the three of you into my boat when I eventually sailed for Rome. But a month ago Brasidas decided upon another round of revision and correction, and frankly, sir, I can stand it no longer. That is why you are about to take the stage."

The Captain remarked that he was not very theatrical.

"I'm sorry," said Homer impatiently, "and I know it is a desperate measure, but I could conceive of nothing else at such short notice. There is no other way to get our hands on a boat."

"A ship!" cried the Captain joyfully.

"Yes indeed," Homer replied. "We need one, if we are to sail away. If you will excuse me, however . . ."

He turned in the saddle – he was a rather awkward rider – and waved his eagle feather. Straightaway, the three scribes rode up. We learned that they were, in fact, professional copyists, trained to write out new copies of books.

"These fellows," Homer explained, "were purchased, at my suggestion, for the copying of the complete *Vindication of Brasidas* next month. But today they have another duty. They will be coaching you on your parts."

"Parts?" demanded Paulla.

"I'm afraid there is no time to argue, madam," said Homer. "You have been cast as Tullia; the Captain here as a druid, a sort of Celtic priest; and this young gentleman as my former master, Lucinus Spurinna. I will be playing myself. We had better hurry – it is only three miles to the villa, and we perform tonight!"

Each of us walked beside one copyist; they had copies of Homer's play. Patiently, my copyist walked me through the role of Spurinna, reading Homer's lines – it seemed that most of my dialogue was with him.

There were three acts. In the first, the Homer character advised me in detail on how to break into the conspirators' house and spy on them. He had a lot to say about the glory of Rome, the vital importance of my mission, and the sad folly of the times.

The second act took place at a dinner party in the house of a superstitious Roman knight. Homer was the guest of honor; Tullia and Spurinna (played by Paulla and myself) were disguised as his slaves, with the Captain on hand as the druid. Here, with delicate philosophical reasoning, expressing the loftiest sentiments, the Homer character convinced the superstitious knight that life was short, that being a traitor was unworthy of a noble soul, and that he should accordingly hand over a vital piece of evidence to the proper authorities.

In the third act, Homer personally led the cavalry to storm the bridge while Paulla and I looked on. He wrestled the druid to the ground and shamed the traitor before an admiring audience of soldiers and mercenaries, who carried him on their shoulders back to Rome.

"Homer," I asked, when I had finished learning my small part, "is this entirely accurate?"

"Accurate, sir?"

"Well, I notice you have all the good lines."

"It is a historical account, sir. I cannot tamper with the truth."

"But what does this play have to do with our ship?"

"Everything, sir."

"What do you mean? No, forget it, we'll trust you. But answer me one question, at least. Who is playing the Roman knight, the traitor?"

"Ah," said Homer with a gleam in his eye, "that part is reserved for Brasidas."

We rehearsed briefly as we walked the last two miles. The sun was already well past noon by the time we caught sight of the sea. It was spread before us like a vast blue shawl stitched with glittering diamonds, folded at the feet of the tall mountains on our left. Our hearts rose. Somewhere past that horizon lay the protection of the law.

The road ran down a gentle slope to the inhabited strip of land by the shore. Here stood the villa and its many out-buildings.

The villa itself was extensive, testifying to Brasidas's great wealth; it must have been quite new, for it was built in the Italian style. At its heart grew an enormous enclosed garden, open to the air and ringed with pillars. On the far side were apartments with marble balconies, looking over the water. A long building, roofed with red tile, contained the owner's offices, library, dining rooms, and kitchens. A little apart, before the storehouses and granaries began, stood a low, flat structure.

"The bathhouse," Homer informed us.

What caught my eye was not the villa itself, however, but the dock. Part of it was built into the shoreline, but one end pushed out into the bay. Two small galleys were moored there. One had a sleek, black prow and sat with its bank of oars tucked in by its sides. The other was more cheerful, painted all in green, resting its oars in the water. I didn't see why we shouldn't make for the boats at once, but Homer instead led us into the villa by a side door. He gave his horse to the copyists and they rode off.

"The theater's on the other side," Homer told us as he ducked inside.

"He has his own theater?" growled the Captain. You could tell he was already working on his stage fright.

The interior corridors were dark after the strong afternoon sun, and the air was musty. Homer led us by a circuitous route, now up a short flight of stairs, now ducking through a busy kitchen. The cooks were aghast at our appearance – we had not washed at all – but a look from Homer silenced them. At last we reached a pair of rooms, empty of furniture but full of babbling people.

"The spare dining rooms," Homer explained as we went

in. "These are the stagehands, and this is the orchestra conductor. Are you ready, then? But where is your chorus, sir?"

"How should I know?" cried the little orchestra conductor, biting his nails. "They've been rehearsing for ten days, and now they leave me for a sniff of air! At a time like this!"

Homer calmed him down and sent someone to find the chorus.

"We're just behind the theater," he said. "Out that door is the stage. You know your cues? Not much more than half an hour left before we – Oh, *hello*, master!" he called in a suddenly cheerful voice, looking past us. Then he whispered, "Keep your heads down."

A voice I dreaded spoke from behind us.

"How does my costume look, Estate Manager?" asked Brasidas. "Do Roman knights really carry these puny round shields?"

Paulla, the Captain, and I stooped a little lower.

"They do carry them, sir, and you look splendid," Homer replied. "Are you sure you know your cues?"

"I know them," barked Brasidas. "But I still think you have all the good lines, Estate Manager. Really," he said darkly, "are you sure this play fully vindicates the cause of Sparta?"

Homer smiled indulgently. "It is a play about justice, sir, eternal justice. It proves that the righteous, like yourself, can only triumph in the end."

"Oh. Well, you know best, I suppose. But I still have some problems with Act Four. Were there really Spartans involved in stopping that conspiracy?"

"Of course there were, sir, just as we pointed out in the *Vindication of Brasidas* several times. They played a vital role."

This seemed to satisfy Brasidas for now, and he departed.

"Act Four?" I whispered to Homer. "I don't have any lines ready for that! We haven't rehearsed!"

"Don't worry, Marcus Oppius," Homer said soothingly. "There is no Act Four."

With the landowner gone, we were quickly turned over to makeup. They exclaimed in horror at our condition and washed our faces. Then they painted black lines on them for eyebrows and thick red around our lips, and we put on the huge (and rather grotesque) acting masks. Paulla seized the chance to remove her wig, which solved the hairdresser's problem of having a blond barbarian playing Tullia; her costume was a yellow robe. All the while the confusion in the room reached greater and greater heights: the stagehands were arguing fiercely, Homer was rebuking the chorus, and a flute-player walked straight through the scenery screen for Act Two. From the open door came the noise of an audience settling down. Paulla, the Captain, and I took refuge in a corner.

"Is this insane?" I asked. "Has he finally gone mad?"

"It looks like it," Paulla agreed. "But then, you have to admit, he's a fairly ingenious fellow."

"Do you think the crowd will be big?" groaned the Captain.

At last, Homer called for silence. He straightened his shirt, moistened his eyebrows, and strode through the open stage door.

At once the noise from the audience ceased. Then they began clapping, louder and louder, and chanting Homer's name. We heard him begin to speak.

"Thank you, thank you. No, please, thank you very much. As you know, I come to you direct from Rome." Some polite clapping at this. "It has been my privilege," he went on, "to work, these past months, with a remarkable man: Brasidas of Sparta, your host this evening and a great patron of the tragic stage. As I'm sure you know, the man is entirely innocent, and it is our pleasure to present a play this evening which amply establishes – nay, which conclusively proves – that the innocent must triumph in the end." Some more applause at this, rather forced. "I give you, ladies and gentlemen, without further ado, *The Conspiracy at Rome*: the exploits of that great Roman hero, that lifelong admirer of Sparta –"

"Give us your tambourine act!" called a voice from the crowd.

"Aulus Lucinus Spurinna. We begin with Act One!"

That play was a shambles. The chorus was drunk, the audience was insolent, and the music was more than a little off-key. If everyone hadn't been terrified of Brasidas – who was, after all, appearing in a leading role – I'm sure we would have been egged. The Captain, faced with two hundred skeptical faces in the rising bank of seats, forgot everything and began roaring in his strange language: fortunately this was perfect for his part. Paulla was excellent as Tullia, though she indulged in some gentle parody of her friend. The crowd actually clapped when she appeared again for Act Three. Homer they tolerated, or rather endured. He got entirely caught up in the moment and began inventing even more lines for himself, including an impromptu panegyric of Brasidas. The landowner himself was a wooden actor, totally unable to convey any emotion except suppressed rage – which I'm sure is what he was feeling in the circumstances of the botched play. But the greatest shame was reserved for me: not because I couldn't hold my own on stage, but because Homer had pared the Spurinna part down to next to nothing. This disappointed the audience. They had come, after all, to watch a hero.

"That's not what Spurinna would say!" claimed one old lady in the back.

"You call that ancient Roman virtue?" cried a well-dressed man in the front row, after the Homer-dominated bridge scene. "Where's the *real* Spurinna?"

After each episode, the musicians took over and we

had a break offstage. Paulla and I spent the first one trying to reassure the Captain, but after Act Three Homer drew us aside.

"It's going splendidly!" he said with satisfaction. "Don't you feel just like you were back in Rome?"

We glared at him. The Captain declared that his acting mask was itching.

"That reminds me," Homer said, "time to exit, stage right."

Signaling for silence, he pointed to the door through which we had first entered. We dropped our masks and ducked out, one by one. Homer joined us soon afterwards.

"I just told the conductor to give them a double helping of the chorus," he chuckled. "Never say I don't understand revenge!"

"What about Brasidas and his guards?" I demanded.

"That's the whole point, sir," Homer informed me, as he led us back through the villa. "He's onstage with all his men! I said we needed fifty soldiers for the grand finale – all the guards on the estate, except at the plantation. He's even had to bring in more from the neighbor's estate. That's the neighbor's green galley moored at the dock. Brasidas' own galley is empty, and the coast is clear!"

I noticed we were taking quite a different route through the corridors and passageways. This time, we cut straight across the garden and then past an interior court with a fountain, under a low arch, and into the pottery workshop.

There we found three cloaked figures waiting: Homer's copyists. They were carrying some twenty-one scrolls, seven apiece.

"Have you got it?" Homer whispered.

"It's the only copy," one of them answered. "Twenty-one volumes."

From the workshop we passed quietly outside, by the quarry. We smelled the sea strongly, though the breeze was blowing down from the highland. A narrow footpath led across the grass to the dock, and we avoided the main route from the villa gates.

Suddenly, as we approached the dock, a man's voice broke the silence.

"Shouldn't you fellows be onstage?"

A well-dressed slave was sitting in the shadow of a cypress tree near the shore end of the dock, scarcely to be seen. He rose slowly and stretched. Homer spun round and didn't miss a beat.

"Ah, it's the manager of our dear neighboring estate!" he cried. "My dear fellow, just the man I was looking for! There's a crisis: we need more actors for the grand finale, and I've been sent to ask you to send your galley crew up to the theater. Right away, if you please."

The man sniffed. "Grand finale, eh? Well, grand finale or no grand finale, I can't send them all."

"Half of them, then."

The man hesitated. It seemed a bizarre request, doubt-less. But Homer certainly looked convincing as a theater manager at his wit's end, so at length he agreed. We walked behind him to the end of the dock, where the galleys were moored. He hastened up the gangplank of the green galley and from inside we heard orders given and obeyed. There was a sound of shuffling feet, and half the oars at the galley's side went slack.

At that moment, we heard the howling of hounds. The echo of an uproar reached us from the direction of the theater.

"By Zeus!" cried Homer. "Everybody get onboard! This is it!"

Scrolls in hand, the copyists rushed up the gangplank of the black-prowed galley: it was indeed deserted. Paulla followed after them, and I followed Paulla. The Captain hesitated on the dock and then turned to help Homer with the heavy mooring cables.

"Get the sail ready!" he called up to me. "Take hold of the halyard!"

I had no idea what a halyard was, but there was a rope attached to the sail. I tried heaving, but it was no use. Paulla dragged the copyists to help and grabbed the end herself.

"Heave!" she shouted.

The yard rose halfway up the mast, the sail with it, and with another great effort it nearly reached the top. The galley's sail was square-rigged, unlike the huge lateen sail of the old *Star of Carthage*; but already we felt the tug of the breeze and the ship strained against the last mooring ropes.

"Don't forget the steering oar!" cried the Captain from the dock. I ran to it while the others raised the anchor.

Just as I reached the steering oar, there was a tremendous crash of noise and the dockside gates of the villa burst open. Men came streaming in our direction. From fifty yards away on the galley I seemed to see each face distinctly. They were all angry, but one face, with its eyebrows blacked thickly and its lips ruby-red, was exploding with murderous fury.

"Betrayed!" screamed Brasidas. "Betrayed by that Hesiod-loving Athenian scum!" He had a sword in his hand; the evening sun glinted on its razor edge and on the spear-tips of the guards behind him. They sprinted down the dock.

There was still one more mooring cable attached. Homer flung himself madly for it; but the Captain turned to face our foes.

"Don't do it!" I shrieked, as he advanced against them.

Homer unlashed the final rope. A guard flung his spear at him but missed, barely. With the movement of the ship, the gangplank was at a crazy angle, but Homer flew up it like a rope-walker, reaching the top as it dropped into the water.

The Captain faced the charge like a lion. He was un-armed, but even as Brasidas slashed with his sword, slicing the shoulder, the Carthaginian picked him up at the waist and spun him round like a piece of ship's timber. He knocked two guards down and the rest faltered. Then he threw Brasidas into the sea.

The splash was enormous, for the Spartan was still in his stage armor. That detail preserved us. The sight of their master flailing in the water, clad in what seemed like heavy bronze, made for little hesitation. A dozen guards threw down their spears and leapt in after him. The Captain, clutching his shoulder, picked himself up and ran to the end of the dock.

The ship was already twenty feet away. He couldn't make it. Instead, he dove in headfirst.

"A rope, toss him a rope!" I yelped.

But Paulla was ahead of me. Before I had spoken, she had tossed a rope for the Captain to grab on to. He was a strong swimmer, luckily, as he'd shown in the shipwreck. Even with his wound, he reached the end of it and hung on for dear life.

Then it was our turn to heave again. Or rather, every-one's turn but mine, since I held fast to the steering oar. Slowly I managed to point the prow toward the open waves.

8

The Manuscript

Darkness saved us. The wind from the highland grew stronger as the sun set. We were aware of frantic calls and shouts on the dock behind as they made ready to follow us; but with half the other galley's crew unloaded and an enraged landowner to save from drowning, they were greatly delayed. Moreover, they had no light to see us by. The last half-circle of the orange sun dipped beneath the horizon as we reached the mouth of the bay, and the green galley behind was only beginning to set sail. Soon the villa was no more than a strip of dim light on the shore, slowly receding as we were carried, again, across the black Aegean Sea.

Once the sail was steady and the steering oar lashed firmly in place, we turned to the poor Captain. He refused to go below. With some cushions from Brasidas' cabin, we propped him up on the poop deck beside the steering oar, and we cut away his grimy shirt.

It was a horrible cut, but it had not reached the bone.

Thick wine-red blood bubbled up from inside. One of the copyists took a look and addressed Homer.

"If you please, sir," said he, "I can help, I hope. My former master was a doctor, and often I have seen him treating such wounds. We must wash the cut immediately with wine and stitch it up."

Paulla washed it – she didn't flinch. She reassured the Captain that it was all right, in fact it was quite normal for the hero to recover from a sword cut, while we ransacked the ship's stores for a needle. I found one in what I took to be the sailmaker's chest.

"It's rather large," said the copyist doubtfully, when he saw it. "Bring a lamp: my master always burned the needle first, to restore the element of heat."

For thread we unpicked strands of rope. The Captain, who was determined not to cry out and thus provide our pursuers with a clue to our position, merely remarked that he would have a tremendous scar. Then he bit on a cord and endured the stitching in the lamplight.

When the slave had finished, I was sure the Captain must have fainted. There had been muscles to sew together as well as skin. But to my astonishment he spoke to me.

"You, Marcus Oppius," he gasped faintly. "You must steer us."

"I have the steering oar lashed, sir."

"No!" whispered the Captain. "You are too . . . too far into the wind. Point the prow . . . more southward."

I wasn't sure where south was, but I kept turning until the Captain spoke again.

"There!" he called. "Keep it steady. If the wind backs . . ." He fell silent.

"If the wind backs?" I asked.

"Then . . . ease the clew and . . . try to keep this course."

With that, he passed out. Before long, I heard him snoring fitfully on the cushions beside me.

I stayed by the steering oar. My hope was that the wind would not back (though how would I know if it did?) and thus I would not have to decipher the Captain's instructions. In spite of the fact that I had never been at sea before Gaius sent me on this doomed mission, I was apparently the most nautical person aboard.

The others, meanwhile, ransacked the ship. Or rather they went systematically through the stores and the two cabins. The galley was hardly roomier than the old *Star of Carthage*, and much narrower, but somehow they managed to find us more candles, clean clothing, a fine red cloak (which Paulla brought out to me on deck), combs, and even hair oil. Nor would we starve. Besides the bread ration for the rowing slaves, Homer discovered a whole pantry of dainties: a jar of honey, a strong red wine, a basket of fresh-picked plums, and (Paulla's delight) real Roman fish sauce. With every discovery they would call softly back to me.

"Marcus, come and see! You'll never believe it! Cheese!"

"I can't," I replied. "I'm steering!"

"Marcus Oppius," cried Homer. "Look at this. Walnuts!"

"Save some for me!" I cried.

Homer emerged with a bucket, which he lowered into the water; then he carried it back down to the cabin. After a while Paulla reappeared. She had managed to put on a dress and a pair of earrings.

"Really, Marcus," she commented, "you still look like a farm slave! What have you been doing all this time?"

I left her with the steering oar and stern advice to rejig the bunts if the wind shifted, and went below.

There was a basin of cold water in Brasidas's cabin. In the dark, I washed my head and neck and put on some oil (for my hair had grown over my ears during our months on the plantation). Finally, I stripped off my foul shirt and found a replacement of new white wool.

Coming out, I met Homer at the cabin door. He held a candle and a sheet of papyrus.

"Sir!" he said eagerly. "Did you know the name of this vessel? I can show you with this document." He held it up and showed me. "The *Spartan Swallow*, sir."

I suppose that, when you are a student of the Muses, such things weigh heavily on your mind.

"It won't do, sir," he began. "Not only is a swallow a very unwarlike bird, but I myself have had enough of Sparta for a lifetime! With your permission, I will rename the ship appropriately."

So, by midnight, after Homer had performed an appropriate sacrifice to Neptune (he made do with plums) on the prow, we were suddenly sailing in the good ship *Hesiod*.

I have called it a galley, and so it was: its natural means of propulsion was a bank of twelve oars on either side. These were now drawn in, of course, in the absence of its crew, and the *Hesiod* was propelled only by the wind. The hull had the same proportions as a real trireme warship, being perhaps five times as long as it was broad. At the bow it was equipped with a blunt ram for striking other ships in battle. There was no lower deck to speak of, merely a narrow hold beneath the main deck. The rowing benches lined the space between the raised poop deck (with its canopy and steering oar) at the stern and the raised boarding deck at the bow. The boarding deck itself was empty, except for a sheet of sailcloth.

Homer, meanwhile, was not content with renaming the ship and continued to explore the hold. Just before dawn, he woke me from a nap in Brasidas's cabin, which I had snatched for a few hours while Paulla briefly took the steering oar. I groaned.

"Don't you ever sleep?" I demanded.

"I'm sorry, sir, but look!" He went to the door and dragged in a heavy satchel. It contained about twenty long cylindrical sticks, perhaps three feet long, tipped with metal.

"Bolts!" he exclaimed with excitement. "Bolts, sir, for a ballista!"

I followed him up on to the boarding deck. He threw back the sailcloth which had been lying there. In the light of the lamp I saw it had covered a great crossbow, four feet wide and six feet long. This was Homer's most triumphant find: a piece of seaborne artillery.

"What kind of pleasure galley is this?" I asked. "Who is this landowner, an amateur pirate?"

The ballista could only be meant for firing at other ships. I had seen them demonstrated by the army when I was a boy, though this naval version was smaller. Still, it could hurl a heavy bolt two hundred yards with incredible force. You put the bolt in a grooved slot, winched back the cord, pointed it, and pulled a lever, releasing the torsion power.

"Do you know how to use one of these?" I asked Homer dubiously.

"Of course not, sir, but the essential principle is clear. This one merely needs to be assembled, I assure you."

We located the metal pivot into which you had to screw the ballista frame, and I went back to the steering oar. Paulla, when she heard the news, looked interested and went forward to watch Homer work.

The dawn came: first my sudden awareness that I could see the bow from my station at the oar, then the faint blue of the east. Soon I could tell there was a mass of land between us and the sunrise.

"By Baal," came the Captain's voice, "that's Cythera!"

He was blinking and stretching his neck where he lay. Tenderly, he felt his shoulder. No more blood was leaking from the cut.

"It's Cythera, my lad!" he repeated. "We've come thirty miles, I think. We must have rounded Cape Tanaerum in the dark. So that's where we've been. As plain as my beard!"

The Captain felt his beard, as though to reassure himself it was still there.

"Well done, my son, well done!" he went on. "You're a natural. We must pass between Cythera and the Donkey's Head, and so north to the Saronic Gulf. Put her over to leeward, that's right. You've a steady hand."

All eyes were turned to Cythera, still distant, but distinct against the rising light. One of the copyists began to sing. But Paulla's keen glance took in the full horizon.

"Marcus!" she gasped. She was pointing astern.

Turning, we saw an incredible sight. Far off, but entirely too near, was a dark shape. Yet we had not passed any little islands on that empty sea.

"A whale, perhaps?" said Homer hopefully.

"Brace the sail!" I cried. "It's the other galley!"

Everyone but the Captain ran to adjust the sail. We would take full advantage of the wind. We even poured water on it to enhance the thrust of the breeze. But we all knew that the other galley had a sail as well. It also had twenty oarsmen.

Two copyists volunteered to row and each grabbed an oar. Homer, Paulla, and I put our heads together.

"Can we land on Cythera?" I suggested.

Homer was against it. Who could say, he argued, whether Cythera would be any more friendly than Laconia?

"Could we outmaneuver them, like in *The Twice-Told Tale*?" asked Paulla.

"This isn't a novel!" I reminded her. "Without oarsmen, we can't outmaneuver anything, and they can spin around in circles if they like."

Even as we debated, however, we saw that neither landing nor maneuvering would be possible. The enemy galley was already gaining ground, cheered perhaps at the sight of its quarry. A few minutes later, we could see the splash of its twenty oars. They would keep straight for us, trying to ram the *Hesiod* in the middle of its side and sink us. We were helpless prey.

Already, with the light rising fast, we could make out the green prow of the pursuing ship. It was coming up fast. The sail was lit by the morning sun, and the oars rose as one, dipped, and raked the foam. They were nearly at battle speed, I reflected, and rather more efficient than our two copyists.

Paulla and the third copyist hurried forward to the ballista. Homer disappeared below. I angled the steering oar to starboard, buying us another minute, but the enemy galley lost no time in changing course to intercept. They were a mere three hundred yards away, coming in at an angle from the starboard side.

Wham! went the ballista on the boarding deck. Paulla had pulled the lever and sent a missile hurtling through the morning air. She missed by a long mark but quickly had another bolt ready in the groove. Together, she and the copyist turned the two-handed crank.

Wham! went the ballista once more. They had adjusted the angle, but too far down. The bolt fell short and skimmed the surface of the sea.

From the starboard rail of the *Hesiod* came a crash and a tinkle of scattered splinters. The enemy galley was shooting back! Before Paulla could send a third bolt at them, we took a second hit, and then a third.

"They must have more than one of those machines!" I shouted.

"Put the helm to port," said the Captain softly. "Buy us a bit more time."

It was only a reprieve, however. Being so much faster, the enemy simply drew even with us and then, with a flourish of his oars, spun round to speed ever closer, again making for our helpless starboard side.

Wham! This time Paulla hit them. The bolt struck the green galley on the prow. But it had no effect: the shaft simply exploded into splinters, not even sticking in the target's hull. The reason was simple. The bolt was bare wood, without its metal tip.

The green galley was level with us now, and closing at an alarming angle. The sea hissed as the deadly ram cut through the waves, just below the waterline. At the prow we could see Brasidas himself, wearing his red cloak and waving a naked sword. Beside him stood another noble-man – the very one who had heckled my performance – Brasidas's friend, the owner of the green galley. They were Paulla's targets.

"Give up!" bawled Brasidas. "You can't run! Give up my galley, or every one of you will perish!"

At that moment, with the enemy no more than thirty yards away, the oars suddenly backed water and the green galley slowed sharply.

Paulla's answer was a last *Wham!* of the ballista, but in her excitement she missed completely, and the bolt sailed off into the sky.

"If that is your choice . . ." Brasidas began.

But then Homer appeared on deck. He was carrying the satchel again, but this time it contained no ammunition.

"Wait!" Homer shrieked out at the green galley. "Sink us at your peril!"

He lifted the satchel above his head for all to see. It was stuffed with twenty-one papyrus scrolls.

"This bag holds the only copy of the *Vindication of Brasidas*!" Homer shouted. "And that is not all: it also con-tains six ballista tips of iron! It will go straight to the bottom!"

"No! No! You lie!" cried Brasidas from across the water, but his sword fell to his side. "That manuscript is safe in my study at home!"

"Do you want proof?" asked Homer. "Shall I read to you?" He rifled in the satchel and produced a scroll. "Let me see, yes, Book 15: '*And a Spartan never yet broke his sworn word, as my enemies in their insolence have dared to assert.*' Or again . . .'"

"It's true!" moaned Brasidas to his friend. "That Athenian swine has my book!" They exchanged a few words. "We shall board you, thieves!" he returned. "We will take what is rightfully mine!"

Homer yielded not an inch. "You will need divers if you want these!" he cried, flourishing a scroll in each hand. "You will never return to Sparta! Your name will never be cleared!"

"Traitor!" shrieked Brasidas. "And you call yourself a publisher!"

"You won't be able to call yourself an author after this!"

Brasidas hesitated. He seemed to be squirming inside his own skin. Turning, he stepped deliberately on the knuckles of the nearest rower, who whined loudly.

At last he spun back to Homer with a look of hatred. "What do you want for it?" he shouted hoarsely.

"We want to reach Athens alive."

"All right, you can do that!" conceded Brasidas.

"In this ship!" cried Homer, dangling the satchel over the side. "Swear it!"

"Yes, yes, yes!" shrieked Brasidas, until Homer jerked the manuscript inboard again. "Yes, I swear it, by all my ancestors! By the green vale of Laconia! By the sacred shrine of Lycurgus, I swear you can take the *Spartan Swallow* to Athens! I will follow you no more. Just give me back my treatise!"

"I will do so!" answered Homer grandly. "Send a man over in a boat. But I still think you should rework the introduction, Brasidas. And then, of course, there is the question of the title . . ."

"Will you still publish it?" asked the vanquished Spartan.

"Don't press me," Homer replied. "Yours is not the only *Vindication* I have to consider. There are others, even longer, that deserve my attention."

A boat was lowered from the side of the green galley, and Homer carefully handed the satchel to the rowers. It did indeed look heavy. Brasidas watched the operation anxiously.

"I'll change the title," he called. "I'll quote more Hesiod, if you wish it. I'll . . ."

But by then the boat was inboard again and the green galley was turning round, its owner too disgusted at Brasidas's behavior to remain. The breeze picked up and our ship was carried forward, rapidly separating from the defeated enemy. Paulla delicately unwinched the ballista.

I ran to Homer and picked him up by the waist.

"You're a maniac!" I cried. "A maniac and a genius!"

"Really, sir," he replied, sighing, "I beg you not to confuse my good fortune with Brasidas's stupidity. I have never seen such a craven performance. Did you see how his eyes never left his own book? Not worthy of a tyrant, really, but not uncharacteristic of an author."

The City of Philosophy

We were two days sailing to Athens. On the first, we crossed the Gulf of Argos. Then, with the Temple of Poseidon flickering from Point Sunium like a distant day-star, we sailed the Saronic Gulf to Piraeus, the port of the ancient city.

"Never thought I'd see it again," sighed the Captain, admiring the golden roof of Poseidon from his sickbed of cushions. "Twelve times I've been to port here, but if it weren't for this fellow," he said, indicating the medical copyist, "there'd be no thirteenth."

He had been tended day and night by the copyist and Paulla, who took shifts. They had kept the wound clean and dry, complimented him on his bravery (which, in retrospect, he was quite proud of), and even managed to comb out and trim his beard. Once again, he looked the part of a Carthaginian merchant, navigating from his bed of cushions while I did the steering. He was an excellent teacher.

On our left appeared the island of Salamis, where the old Athenians had fought their great battle against the Persian King. Here we were met by a small boat containing the assistant harbormaster, who hailed us and instructed us to dock in the north harbor. We replied that we had no oarsmen to steer us. He looked puzzled, and then demanded if they had died of plague. When we burst out laughing, he relaxed, but directed us to a rather distant pier where we would not bump into any other ships. It took all the money we had found onboard, except for some small change, to pay the harbor fee.

I was worried that someone would notice the former *Spartan Swallow* and inform on us, but in fact our galley was soon lost amid the hundreds of seacraft in the port. We shortened sail to the minimum and slowly drifted in behind a large, rather mangy merchant vessel. A gang of waterfront slaves was unloading a mountain of jugs from its hold.

The Captain felt strong enough to stand. The medical copyist had rigged a sling for his arm, and he joined us on the wharf.

"Should see my shipping agent," he said gloomily. "Explain about the old *Star of Carthage* and the cargo." He did not sound optimistic.

"Wasn't the cargo insured?" asked Paulla.

"It was," said the Captain. "But he'll be wanting me to take another shipment back west, and I can't do that now."

"Come now, Captain," I broke in, "you're the one who saved us at the villa. Anyway, we're just your passengers. We're all agreed: the galley belongs to you."

"Well, now, that's a terribly generous thing to do," declared the Captain, clapping us on the back. "But even so, a little galley can't take cargo back to Rome."

"You can sell it," I said. "Sell it and buy a new merchantman."

Homer was shocked. "Sell the *Hesiod*?" he exclaimed. "Sell the finest ship in the fleet?"

"What fleet?" I asked. "But that reminds me. Did anyone see Spurinna's trireme in the harbor? The *Rapacious*?"

No one had. There had only been one or two Roman warships there. The rest were presumably out with Admiral Pompey, chasing pirates.

We turned our attention to a more urgent problem: we were flat broke. I would have gone straight to Caesar's agent in Athens, but his name had been lost along with Gaius's sealed letter when Paulla had discarded it from my trunk. I didn't know a soul in Athens.

But Homer, of course, was practically at home. He put Spurinna's manuscript under his arm and rubbed his hands. "I did spend twenty years here, sir," he explained. "And not altogether unprofitable ones. We'll just look up one of my old friends. He'll help me get started in publishing my former master's book."

So, with Homer's copyists in tow, we began our walk up the old road to Athens. Until the Roman siege just twenty-five years before, that road had been lined on either side by the Long Walls, which protected the link between the inland city and its port. These had been knocked down, however, and lay crumbling a little distance from the side of the road. The route was now lined with small shops, catering to tourists. The Athenians had given up resisting Rome and had lately been transforming their city into a university town and tourist attraction. They had replanted the trees (also destroyed during the fighting) and invited various cultured Romans to live among them and help rebuild.

Our first stop was the Agora, the town square. This lay beyond the Hill of the Nymphs, nestled under the Hill of Ares. What with the long walk from the port and the May sunshine, we were sweating by the time we reached it. I was eager to see the sights, for the city was altogether glorious: full of well-dressed people, covered in murals, and crammed with monuments and porticoes. I longed to climb the tall Acropolis and visit the enormous Temple of the Virgin. Seeing Homer's friend was more urgent, however. Homer asked after him in the Agora and got directions to his house.

"My friend Anaxilaus is just the man," he proclaimed as we walked, "even if he does belong to the Pythagorean school. You see, he has developed a philosophy to the effect

that money and open-handed generosity are the straightest ways to truth. An excellent fellow."

As we followed the directions, however, we found ourselves searching through a tangled maze of back alleys. The
farther we went, the seedier the alleys got. Finally, not far
from the Dipylon Gate, we spotted the double palm tree,
which our directions specified. There was a small shack
underneath it that was half collapsing.

"Surely this can't be the place?" I asked.

Homer knocked. The door was opened by a thin,
unwashed, and undernourished man in rags. He was
holding a scroll tightly in one hand, and looked us over
suspiciously. Then he noticed Homer's face.

"Homer!" he exclaimed. "Is it actually you? Are you back
in Athens?"

"I am indeed," replied Homer warmly. "But what has
happened to you, Anaxilaus? Why are you living in a such
a shack?"

"Oh, this," said the thin man, smiling. "Yes. It is my latest
philosophy. It was shortly after you left for Italy, I believe,
and I was speaking with the Epicureans one day. Something they said – it was just an aside, mind you – convinced
me that money and open-handed generosity were the
straightest ways to ignorance." And here he tossed his scroll
to the floor behind his back, as though afraid we might
help ourselves to it.

"But, my dear fellow," protested Homer, "we've come to you for assistance! We have no money at all, and I thought that you might be able to indulge in your former philosophy and help us."

"My dear Homer!" exclaimed Anaxilaus. "How can I help you when, being without money and rather miserly yourself, you are yourself already well advanced on the straightest way to truth?"

"But, my dear Anaxilaus, I have a manuscript in my possession that I have come here to publish. I need money for ink and paper and a place for the copyists to work."

Not to mention food, I thought.

"A manuscript?" inquired Anaxilaus. "Who is it by? Let me see. Oh, it is in Latin, indeed. What's this – the author is Spurinna? Not the same young man who was just here?"

"You've seen him?" asked Paulla eagerly.

"No, indeed, my dear," said the philosopher. "Or only from a distance. The crowds were too thick. Can you believe he captured that pirate ship with so small a crew?"

"Aulus captured a ship . . . !" she said, her eyes glowing.

"But if you want my opinion," said Anaxilaus importantly, "you ought to take this Latin book of yours to Atticus. He's a splendid man. Speaks just like an Athenian. Though, of course, he speaks that barbarian language also."

"Latin?" I asked.

"Just so. He is a Roman aristocrat, after all, even if we consider him one of us."

"Where can we find him?"

Asking directions from Anaxilaus proved to be futile, however, as his new philosophy did not include explanation. Instead, we went straight back to the Agora and inquired after Atticus.

"Why, Atticus," answered one woman at a vegetable stall, "that's a charming man! They tried to make him a citizen here, for all the good things he's done. Don't you know the way?"

She told us to look for a modern house with a red door on the Hill of Mars, by the Temple of the Unknown God. Weary, but eager now to meet a man of whom all spoke so highly, we again ascended the Hill of Mars and searched near the Temple. In the end, we found we had walked right past it twice. It was much more modest than we were expecting, in the best Athenian taste, shaded by cypress trees and set back from the street.

A polite slave answered the door.

"We are Romans," I began, "shipwrecked and wretched, and we ask to see the master of this house."

The slave's mouth curled in amusement and he signaled for us to wait. A minute later we were shown in. From the front, I had expected an entirely Greek interior, and had been wondering what sort of Roman would live in a Greek house. I was relieved to see the front hall adorned with portraits of his ancestors, just like in Rome. In the middle of the courtyard stood a man in a toga, a

Roman knight. I nearly wept to see that garment: it reminded me of my father in his hall in Reate, and even of Gaius in his gentler moods.

He was about forty years old, I decided. His hair showed no gray, but the face was that of a man who knew life well. His green eyes twinkled as he gave us a friendly wave and approached.

"Shipwrecked and wretched, are you?" he inquired with a smile, speaking Latin. "But what may be your names?"

The Captain grunted his name.

"Marcus Oppius Sabinus," I added.

"Aemilia Lepida Paulla," said Paulla with downcast eyes.

"Aulus Lucinus Homerus," put in Homer.

Atticus's mouth fell open for a moment. Then he closed it and seemed about to speak. Then he merely smiled again. "Well, well," he said with a bow, "I can see there is more to this than you can explain in my courtyard. You are just in time for dinner and that, I think, will solve the first of your problems."

He led us to a dining room at the back of the house. It looked out on a small but colorful garden. The hallways were painted, but not with any elaborate frescoes. Our copyists went off to eat with the household.

"It is always my custom to have some reading at dinner," Atticus said, as we lay down. "With Roman guests, I think we might have a little Latin poetry."

As we ate the simple meal – fish, grilled vegetables, and

seed-cakes, but with lots for everyone – the same slave who had answered the door performed a reading of an epic poem in Latin. It was full of storm and fury, but rather swollen, and I confess I stopped paying attention fairly quickly. Besides, I was famished and preoccupied with the food. I do remember one especially dreadful line – *O luck-borne Rome, when I was consul born!* – which clashed like someone playing the cymbals. The Captain, at least, seemed interested, stroking his beard the whole time and nibbling a seed-cake until he fell fast asleep.

By the time the reader finished, dinner was over and the evening was ending. The slave lit some lanterns and Atticus himself poured us each a modest glass of wine.

"Did you like the poem?" he inquired.

I said it wasn't bad.

Atticus smiled. "It was bad," he confessed. "Or at least, a bit long. But I just received a copy in a letter from my friend, Cicero."

"Cicero?" I was startled. Had I been dining at the enemy's table?

"Yes," said Atticus, "and I'm afraid he's the author of the poem. Would you think a man so eloquent could write verse like that? There was one line in particular – *O luck-borne Rome, when I was consul born!* – which I think must be a copyist's mistake."

I laughed and said that I too had noticed that particular verse.

Atticus smiled. "But now we come to even stranger things," he said. "I am amazed to find I am dining with the daughter of my friend Lucius Aemilius Lepidus Paullus, the freedman of that remarkable young fellow Spurinna, and a young man from the Sabine country, judging by your name. As well, of course, as with my honored Carthaginian guest." The Captain was snoring gently. "Now, I would be fascinated if just one of you appeared at my door, but all three together is quite remarkable. Please tell me your tale."

We told it to him in full. I carried the main story, Paulla leapt in frequently to correct me, and Homer enlarged on various incidents with a telling poetic quotation. The stars were twinkling by the time we finished.

"Where is this precious memoir of Spurinna's?" asked Atticus, when we were through. Homer produced it from beneath his shirt, and the Roman took it gingerly. "It's been through a lot," he remarked as he unfolded the scroll, which was indeed a little damp and flattened. "But how do you intend to publish it?"

Homer confessed that he was altogether penniless.

"Yes, I see that. Well, for now you must stay here as my guests. No, no, I insist – for a few days at least. If you have a mind to follow after Spurinna" – and here Paulla's eyes came alive – "then I won't set any guards at your door: at least not at yours, my dear girl. They wouldn't survive."

Paulla took a quick breath.

"Yes," Atticus went on with a smile, "I had news about such things two months ago. They are searching every inch of Italy for you, I believe. Some people are saying it is all a wicked plot by Caesar to kidnap you in exchange for your clan's votes."

Paulla began to correct him, but Atticus just smiled.

"Of course, I realize it was your own doing," he said, "and rather rash of you, if I may say. I will mention that you are safe when I next write to Cicero; he will reassure your family. They will certainly send for you, but for the time being at least, all of you should rest. Shipwrecked and then three months on a plantation – why, by Hercules, I would never believe it if I read it in a novel! The Captain here needs careful tending, but I can provide that. The best doctor in Athens owes me a favor."

We expressed our sincere gratitude for his kindness.

"Please," said Atticus, blushing slightly, "there is no need to thank me. I too, am a guest in Athens, you know, though I have been here twenty years. The hard part is trying to leave. But tomorrow you will see more of the place, I hope."

We spent nine glorious days in the city of philosophy. The first day, as we took a bite of bread together before he was obliged to meet his morning visitors, Atticus spoke with me, and I told him about myself.

"If you like speeches," he said, "this is your city. Why don't you go down to the Painted Porch and hear the orators?"

The three of us went together; the Captain was being treated by Atticus's friend the doctor. It was hot for May, with a sweep of cloud across the north. Life in the street seemed different than it was in Rome, though hardly less noisy. Many more women were veiled, and everyone walked. There was not a sedan-chair to be seen. Half the men wore beards, not bushy like the Captain's but trimmed quite short. Students, staring at their feet, wandered past with scrolls stuck under their arms. Vagabonds slept in the open, until you realized, when they woke up and began discoursing, that they were actually members of an open-air philosophical movement. There were few togas to be seen, except on some young Romans who were hurrying, like ourselves, to hear the orators. Atticus had lent me a toga, but Homer said he preferred a simple shirt while he was on his old stomping grounds.

"There's that old fellow," he said, pointing to a beard in the crowd, "still hawking those old doctrines! By Zeus, is it possible? And there's Anaxilaus with his miserly new philosophy. Hallo there, Anaxilaus!"

The philosopher joined us as we reached the Painted Porch on the north side of the Agora. This was a huge open colonnade with a tall roof and famous paintings on the inside. On one end, a group had gathered facing the outside marble wall. A man was just walking up the few steps that raised him above the level of the crowd. I didn't catch his name.

"Quickly, let's find a place," I muttered.

The man began to speak. He started with a bit of light humor about Alexander the Great – "Is Alexander in the crowd? No? Good!" – and then addressed us. He was pretending to be Alexander the Great urging his army to fight bravely. I laughed at first – for the man was plainly not Alexander the Great – and then found myself swept away by his words. The future of Greece was at stake, he proclaimed. Yes, there was the danger of death, and death was certainly fearsome. But more fearsome was the death of a friend, and more fearsome still was the death of a country. Beside the element of danger, there was the hope of glory; beside the possibility of defeat, there was the chance of victory. Indeed, the gods might take victory for granted – for they are all-powerful – but today we mortals must seize hold of it before the sun sets. He urged us to take pity on the enemy, who were facing us unaware that fate was on our side. He reminded us that our ancestors were looking on, trembling that we might lose. And he declared that this was the final battle, and all we had won before would be for nothing if we failed, and everything in the world would be ours if we triumphed. He himself would be there beside us, fighting in the front rank.

There were tears in my eyes by the time the man finished. I saw myself literally holding a pike and glaring across the battlefield. The speaker was no longer, in my mind, a rather short Athenian but instead a magnificent young king on horseback, gesturing with his sword to the horizon and proclaiming that the universe was his. I cheered at every full stop.

As the man left the steps, to great applause, Homer nudged me in the ribs.

"Sir, all this battling makes me hungry."

"Homer, I had no idea a speech could be like that! Did you hear him? It was like he was a different person! What fire! What emotion!"

"Yes, sir, there is something to be said for oratory."

I looked around me. I was still in the same Agora, still at the Pointed Porch. But suddenly I understood something I had never learned from all those speeches in class. It wasn't about the words on the page anymore: at least, it didn't have to be just that. I felt rather embarrassed at my old performances in school, or in front of my parents. But I knew that I could do it too, if I got a chance.

I turned around to tell Paulla. She wasn't there.

"Oh, yes, sir, she and Anaxilaus departed. They've gone to listen to the philosophers in the shade. They declared it was too hot to stand here."

Regardless of the weather, I was entranced. I spent all day listening, imagining what courage it must take to get up in front of such a critical audience. The Athenians, however, did it very calmly. Eight or nine speakers gave their speeches, most on a historical subject, and the effect was the same each time. I could well picture what such men must have been like before the Romans came, when those fiery speeches were for real. At last, Homer dragged me away to eat.

So our days passed. My parents, I reflected, would be quite pleased that I was really in Athens, learning from the very best – how different it was from sleepy Reate! Eventually I could show off what I'd learned to Gaius, maybe even impress Caesar himself! Meanwhile, the Captain recovered slowly under the doctor's care, and Homer got into dozens of arguments with old friends. As for Paulla, she visited the philosophers every day, wandering off with one of Atticus's female slaves to sit under the trees, even as far off as the old Academy outside town. Each evening she looked a little more thoughtful, less like a silly girl and more like a young Roman woman.

"I didn't think I'd like it at first," she confessed, when I grilled her about her philosophizing one afternoon. "At first I just went to laugh at them. But the thing is, Marcus, none of these philosophers are alike. Some of them are just buffoons, like Anaxilaus, but some are quite serious. And even with those, some are gentle, and some are very cold, and with some you feel like you're talking to your grandfather. And they listen to you, even if you're just a girl – well, sometimes."

"You mean, even if you're going to be a powerful Roman lady someday."

"Oh no, Marcus, it's not like that. To them, we're just a sort of barbarian, you know." She grinned. "But they don't care, and they don't mind when you disagree with them. Take that Zeno of Sidon, for instance. Yesterday he was going on about how romantic love is the only real kind there is, and I put up my hand and I said, 'Zeno, that's not true, there are other kinds. What about love of your country?' The students all laughed at this, of course – a typical Roman question, they said. But I stuck to my argument. I said, 'Well, what about love of your family, Zeno? What about love of your friends?' Because loyalty is real love too, isn't it, Marcus?"

"You're missing your family," I said.

"No!" she said fiercely. "That's not it. They can rot in Rome, for all I care," which didn't strike me as a very philosophical thing to say.

On the ninth day of our stay in Athens, Atticus summoned us to his study.

"I've just had another letter from my friend Cicero," he said. "Not much in it, mostly the usual gossip, but there is one thing." He read from the letter:

"'*My people have found out that Caesar has sent an agent to Greece to keep Pompey away from me. We*

don't know who, but it might be that Spanish officer I
wrote to you about before. In your previous letter, you
told me that Pompey has scattered his fleet looking for
the last pirates, so there is nothing to prevent him from
returning to Italy at once. Be a friend and send him the
enclosed note immediately.'"

Atticus looked up. "I must do this for Cicero: he is my best
friend. Let me say it right now. I want you to take his note
to Pompey for me. I trust you, and I would appreciate it."

"Of course," I said automatically. "I've been your guest
for nine days. I can hardly refuse."

Neither could I refuse, I thought, to get my hands on
that note. Suddenly I had visions of fulfilling my mission
for Gaius after all. He had declared that Cicero and
Pompey must not join forces, and here was Cicero proposing exactly that.

"I would go," the Captain said. "I'm well now. But my
galley has no oarsmen."

"I'll provide them," said Atticus, "at my expense. In
exchange, I'll borrow the copyists, if you don't mind. There
are one or two books I would like to borrow from my
friends and have copied out."

"Wait a minute," interrupted Homer. "The copyists
belong to me. *I* stole them. If you want someone to take the
letter, I shall go! Spurinna is my former master, and he is
with Pompey."

"If Spurinna's there, I think *I'm* the natural choice," volunteered Paulla softly.

Atticus chuckled. "Four candidates, then? Indeed I'm touched by your friendship. As a matter of fact, I was hoping you would all go together. These spies of Caesar's – you must be careful, and watch each other's backs. Beware of any Spanish Romans you meet. No one must know what Cicero hopes to arrange with Pompey. It would wreak havoc with the plans of all good men."

As he thanked us once again, I thought, *Well, Gaius, wreaking havoc with the plans of all good men is your specialty, not mine. But no doubt Caesar will be extremely grateful.*

10

The Cilician Sword

It was with some trepidation that I boarded the *Hesiod* once again. Our two previous voyages – the first ending in shipwreck, the second starting with our escape from the villa – had not been tranquil. Nonetheless, I felt the burden of my secret mission. If I could only frustrate Cicero's plans with Pompey, Gaius would certainly overlook my delays. Part of me even wished I was back in Reate, where they never sent you on secret missions.

We were headed for Samos, the large island on the eastern side of the Aegean. Atticus had told us that Admiral Pompey was using Samos as his supply depot during the campaign against the pirates in those waters, though his ships were mostly out hunting for them.

Our host had been generous in equipping us. He hired twenty free men to serve as rowers. It was a tradition at Athens not to use slaves as rowers on the galleys, and the port was full of unemployed people who were happy to serve. He also purchased new clothes for us: togas for

Homer and me, a costly Phoenician robe for the Captain, and a new silk dress and matching veil for Paulla. Foreseeing a meeting with Spurinna, she had even borrowed money and gone to the most talented hairdresser in Athens. She was now wearing her hair pinned up in the Greek style. Space was again limited on the little *Hesiod*, but we took shifts in the cabins. Fortunately, the voyage this time would be short.

Homer had entrusted Spurinna's memoir to Atticus and the copyists. In its place, he was now carrying Cicero's note to Pompey inside his shirt. I spent most of the trip to Samos trying to get a look at it. Unfortunately, the Greek had evidently decided that Caesar's secret agent might have infiltrated the Athenian crew and consequently he felt honor-bound never to allow it off his person. I tried asking his opinion of its literary style, to get him to read it to me, but he informed me superciliously that it was "doubtless in the very best taste." I tried getting him to demonstrate the workings of the ballista to me, which I thought might require him to remove the letter from his clothing, but he preferred to explain the ballista from the comfort of his hammock. I even tried slipping into the cabin while Homer was asleep, but his tasteless snoring made me nervous, and the scroll I grabbed from the side of his bed proved to be no more than an astronomical treatise in verse. After that I gave up. All I could do, I decided, was to keep my eyes open and hope to interfere with Cicero's plans on Samos. But time was running out.

So, in style, and with intrigue in the air, we coasted through the Cycladic Isles. First, we rounded Point Sunium, waving good-bye to Poseidon's temple, and passed between Ceos and Cynthus. We went east past Syros, and saw Delos, the Holy Island, and the beaches of Mykonos gleaming in the sunset. That night we crossed the open waters until, at dawn, we found Icaria off the port bow. We followed its steep edge to the eastern tip. From there it was an afternoon's sail, along Thymaina and Corassia, to Samos itself. The island was large, however, and the Captain decided we would travel around the north side to the city and its ancient harbor. The free rowers were proving their worth. The *Hesiod* was cutting through the choppy waves like a real warship.

Paulla was the first to spot the fleet. As soon as we sighted Samos, she took station on the bow, with her veil blown back like some sea goddess from the days when nymphs and satyrs inhabited these shores. She knew it, too, and she was confident that Spurinna, for his part, would be gazing westward from the prow of the Roman flagship and would, therefore, behold her at her best. She gave a shout and pointed at the mouth of Samos harbor ahead of us.

"Carry on, Captain!" she called. "We're nearly there!"

There were a dozen warships lying at anchor at the mouth of the bay, and we were rapidly approaching. Besides the flagship, which was a tall quinquereme with immense oars, there were four triremes and seven biremes. It seemed that Pompey's fleet was not dispersed after all. Perhaps he was preparing for a new operation and would not be able to return to Italy. We lowered our sail and came in under oar power.

"I didn't know Rome still had any quinqueremes," I said to Homer.

"Perhaps they've bought one out here," he answered.

We coasted to a halt between one of the triremes and the giant quinquereme. Another trireme moved immediately to our rear. I looked at the marshaled vessels and felt a qualm. Surely it was unusual for Roman warships to be decorated in these gaudy colors, each with a toothy mouth painted onto its bow like a ravening shark's maw. It didn't say much for discipline, and the few seamen staring curiously over the side looked to be an unruly gang – hardly Roman officers.

"Ahoy, there, little galley!" called a voice from the quinquereme, towering twenty feet above us.

"Ahoy!" called the Captain from the poop deck. But I saw him looking nervously at the trireme which had taken station behind us. *Not much of a welcome*, I could see him thinking.

"Ahoy!" I called from the Captain's side. "We have come with news for Admiral Pompey. May we come aboard?"

The man who had hailed us did not reply for a moment.
He stared briefly; he was wearing a yellow handkerchief
over his hair. Then he vanished from the side, and soon a
different person appeared, taking hold of the rigging with
one foot on the rail. He was wearing a Cilician cap and had
a long pointed beard, dyed red. It was emphatically not
Pompey the Great.

"I'm Admiral here," he announced in a thick Cilician
accent. "I'll take your news, by Sabazius, and meanwhile it's
we who'll do the boarding!"

With that, a growl went up along the rails of the two
ships on either side. Panic seized our ship and the Captain
shouted frantically to back water; but with the trireme
behind us we had no room to turn around. At that
moment, half a dozen ballista bolts impacted all along our
hull, and one struck the poop deck beside me. The Captain
roared and cursed: a huge splinter had stuck inside his
lower leg. Grappling hooks came sailing through the air,
snagging our rigging, and the quinquereme's oars were
drawn in on the side facing us. The *Hesiod* was pulled
sideways toward it, into the shade of the giant galley's top
deck. Shirtless men with knives in their belts and ban-
danas on their necks tumbled to the *Hesiod*'s deck and
sprang up with fire in their eyes. They were undoubtedly
merciless pirates.

"We surrender!" I shouted hastily. They had us hope-
lessly outnumbered. More pirates had encircled Paulla at

the bow – she had begun to swing the ballista round on them, but they overpowered her. She was shoved back to join us on the poop deck, where the man who had first hailed us took control. He knocked the wounded Captain down and bellowed to his own men.

"Half of you, now, you keep those rowers in their seats – nothing funny, got it? You gentlemen," he said, addressing Homer and me with his best impression of a smile, "can go up that ladder, quickly now! And the lady, of course," he said, with a leer at Paulla, who had lowered her veil again.

Our hearts were beating hard – at least I know mine was – as the three of us were pushed and pulled up a ladder to the main deck of the quinquereme. Even in the bay, the two ships rose and fell on the swell, and it was hard not to look down at the chasm of seething sea beneath the ladder's frail rungs. At the top we were hauled up by both armpits and made to stand in a little group. The self-proclaimed Pirate Admiral was there, and he laughed at us heartily.

"One . . . two . . . three Roman birds caught in our cage!" he counted, chuckling at our discomfort. Homer's toga had slipped off his shoulder and he did look pitiful. I saw that the Pirate Admiral's face was covered with the scars of vicious combat. He was a huge man, middle-aged, but showing every sign of immense physical strength.

"Our Captain is wounded!" Paulla protested shrilly. "One of your bolts hit his leg. Bring him up, he needs a doctor!"

"Well, if that isn't the way to lecture your captors!" exclaimed the Pirate Admiral. "Your captain will come up, don't you worry, along with the rest of your crew." He leaned over the side again and addressed his man in the yellow handkerchief. "Get those rowers up here," he bellowed. "We'll still be shorthanded, but we need 'em. And search the ship!"

Homer, meanwhile, was gyrating surreptitiously where he stood. I knew he was trying to shift Cicero's sealed note from his midriff, where it bulged rather obviously beneath his shirt.

"Can't say I've ever seen this!" said the Pirate Admiral with a grin. "Usually we have to go chasing galleys such as yours, but here you are, coming to us like old friends. Still, I guess you must have thought we *were* your friends, eh, your precious little Roman fleet? Can't blame you! But that Pompey never got so many ships in once place, believe me, as I've got here, and he never set foot on such a flagship as this here *Sword of Cilicia*! You can ask the man himself soon, I'm sure."

"You mean you've got him?" I cried. "Pompey the Great?"

"The Great, is he? No doubt he is, no doubt he is!" laughed the Pirate King. "He can look to revising his titles after we're through with him. But to answer you, he's not here yet, but you can give me your news for him, I'll pass it on."

"No treasure on the galley, Your Honor!" called the man in the handkerchief from the deck of the *Hesiod*.

"You're sure?" growled the Pirate Admiral over the side. "What about jewels?"

"Sure I'm sure," came the reply. "We've torn through it, there's nothing."

"Well," said the Pirate Admiral, returning to us with an angrier glance. "No gold, no jewels, what kind of prize is this?"

Homer replied that gold and jewels were nothing to us, since he, for one, valued modesty above mere worldly wealth.

"Modesty, eh?" spat the Pirate Admiral. "Well, I'm not modest, and neither are these shipmates of mine. Modesty! Ever heard of a modest pirate? But what's that you're hiding in your shirt, then, you great prince of modesty?"

At the pirate's bidding, two sailors seized hold of Homer and a third rifled his clothing. Cicero's note was discovered immediately and shown to the Pirate Admiral.

"Yes, yes," he said as he unrolled it. "No doubt this'll be some of that news for Pompey we've been hearing so much about. Any of you devils read that Latin?" he barked, looking to his crew. One lanky, unshaven fellow volunteered meekly.

"Read it aloud, then!" bellowed the Pirate Admiral.
The lanky pirate broke the seals. This is what we heard:

Atticus to Pompey: Greetings. I am sending these three
people to you, Admiral, along with the note enclosed.
They are Oppius Sabinus, Aemilia Lepida Paulla, and
Lucinus Homerus. The last will be familiar to your
young friend Spurinna; the girl is the daughter of
Aemilius Lepidus Paullus, whom of course you know.
Please give them a friendly welcome and send them
back to me.

"Oh-ho!" cried the Pirate Admiral when he heard this.
"You'll fetch a powerful great ransom, the three of you,
from this! Better than jewels to me!"

Paulla groaned. She was imagining the humiliation of
being ransomed back to her family. But I felt a sudden gust
of fearlessness.

"You would do better to kill us now," I declared to the
Pirate Admiral.

Homer jerked his head at me and began to protest vehemently.

"Eh?" asked the Pirate Admiral with a giggle, ignoring
Homer. "Now why would I do that, when you'll fetch such
a fine bag of gold from your rich friends?"

"Because," I answered in a quavering voice, "if you don't
kill us, we shall track you down!"

There was silence. Then the whole deck burst out laughing. It went on for a while.

"By Sabazius, what a day!" said the Pirate Admiral, wiping the tears of merriment from his red beard. "I wish all prizes were like this! But you," he said, clearing his throat and turning to the lanky crewman, "read the rest."

The unshaven pirate cleared his throat and now read out Cicero's note to Pompey.

Cicero to Pompey: Greetings. Old friend, the time has come for all good men to make alliance. I hear from my young friend Spurinna that you will soon be returning to Italy, for your fleet is scattering, the pirates are subdued, and your glorious campaign is complete. I myself will come to Brundisium to welcome you. We must speak about the Tribunes for next year: Caesar is trying to rig the election, and your votes will make the difference. Come before September. In exchange, I shall organize your Triumph. Farewell.

There was silence on deck. The pirates seemed to be wondering if they had already been subdued, as the letter said. They didn't show much sign of it to me. Weren't we at anchor in the midst of a twelve-ship pirate fleet?

"By the great god Sabazius," the Pirate Admiral swore at last. "Is this a trick? Has he actually scattered his fleet?" He snatched the letter from the lanky pirate and peered at the broken seals, giving us a searching glance. He was still for a moment, his red beard stiff in the sea breeze. Then he swung round to his crew.

"Where did the fisherman say Pompey's flagship was?"

"Making for Miletus, Your Honor!"

"Aye, Miletus. That's where we'll catch him, then! Boys," he proclaimed to the crew, and the other triremes heard the great booming voice as well, "the Roman fleet's scattered! Tomorrow, aye, tomorrow we'll sail, and get our revenge on the Roman Admiral!"

A deafening cheer went up.

"Here's to the Red Beard! Here's to the Admiral!" they called, shouting it from all three decks. "Tomorrow we sail! Tomorrow!"

"As for you guests," said the Pirate Admiral wickedly, "you can watch from the deck while the Romans lose this battle. Fair is fair: it's you that have opened the road to dear Admiral Pompey!"

"No," groaned Paulla softly. "Not poor Aulus!"

"Take them to the brig," rasped the Pirate Admiral, and straightaway six pirates pulled us through the stern cabin door and down a short ladder. Before we entered the smelly darkness of the interior, I caught a glimpse of our rowers being forced up the ladder from the *Hesiod*. The Captain was in front, his face white and his costly robe, now soaked with blood, wrapped tightly round his calf. I don't know if he caught my eye, for we were soon hidden from view, but in my mind I could already see him shack-led helplessly to a pirate oar.

"Here's your fine accommodation!" giggled our escort, opening a low door. Inside were various wooden crates, several large jugs, strings of sausage, and sets of iron shack-les. A small lamp gave off dull light. "Don't go eating the Admiral's dainties, or he'll ransom you half dead!"

They put our hands and legs in fetters, with a familiar chain through the leg cuffs, attaching them tightly to our hands. It was most uncomfortable. We could hear the Admiral celebrating with his shipmates in the cabin above our heads. From far below came a more ominous sound: the shuffling and clanking of our crew being hitched to the quinquereme's oars. They had been pressed to help fill the vast number of hands needed to speed the great vessel in search of its enemies.

"Well, Homer?" I asked, as our jailors departed and we were left alone with our chains. "Any suggestions? Any sign of poetry in that brute's character for you to get a handle on?"

He regarded me coolly from his awkward posture. "I'm quite satisfied at being still alive, sir," he replied, "after your rather precipitous suggestion that we be murdered. Besides, sir, it sounds as though this Pirate King is preoc-cupied with the coming battle."

"What about you?" I asked Paulla. She was twisting herself in a rather bizarre fashion and trying to get her veil off. "Any great ideas from *The Sad Spanish History*?"

At that she bridled, ceased her fidgeting, and looked at me with contempt. "By Juno, Marcus, will you never stop whining? You're fine sometimes, but other times I think you're worse than one of my father's mules! What's the point in having adventures if you only look on the negative side all the time?"

"Maybe you'd like to tell me the positive side of being kidnapped by pirates!"

"I'm making a bigger point!" she said with exasperation. "A *philosophical* point, come to think of it. What I'm saying is, the gods help the brave! They, and I for that matter, haven't got time for the Marcus Oppius School of Pessimism."

"Are you suggesting, madam," inquired Homer, intervening, "that '*Whoever shall against the Titans strive, Jove won't ignore, nor of renown deprive*' as Hesiod expresses it?"

"Probably," Paulla answered impatiently. "I mean, we need to be serious and escape! Think of Aulus! We need to get word to Admiral Pompey. And to answer your initial question, Marcus," she said, calming down and resuming her twisting motion, "I am actually thinking of something in *The Twice-Told Tale* where . . ." She stretched her neck down to her hands and snatched at her pinned-up hair, then gave a cry.

"I've pricked my hand! Come on, Marcus, shuffle over toward me and use your teeth."

"I can't chew through iron," I said sulkily.

"No doubt! You have to get one of my hairpins in your teeth and drop it into my hand, all right? As I was saying, in *The Twice-Told Tale* the heroine manages to escape from the pirates by using her hairpin to undo the cuffs! But I suppose you skipped that part!"

There was nothing for it but to do as she said. I leaned over, bit into the hairbun, and felt the sharp metal hairpin. I was also blasted by a wave of perfume, which she must have applied to her hair liberally before her planned reunion with Spurinna. Gasping, I managed to get my teeth on the head of the pin, and then drew it slowly out from the thick bun. I turned my head, careful not to drop the pin, and let it fall into her outstretched hand.

"There, not bad, Marcus!" she enthused. "I'm sorry I spoke so severely. But you see how useful my novels are, after all?"

As she turned to free Homer's hands and the lock gave a soft click, I had to admit that she had a point. In two minutes we stood stripped of our chains, rubbing our ankles and wrists, buried in the belly of the giant *Sword of Cilicia*. We waited for night to fall and then softly opened the cell door.

11

The Forgotten Isle

Paulla snuffed the bronze lamp inside our prison and grabbed it. We crept under the low door, leaving the heavy togas and Paulla's veil behind. The corridor was deserted. Everything was dark except to our left, farther aft, where a candle, encased in a thick orange glass, hung from the deckhead. By its glow we could see a hatchway at the end, with a steep stairway plunging below. Men were moaning underneath us: the galley slaves, presumably, sleeping fitfully at their oars. Yet the sound seemed to come from the ship itself, not from the downward opening.

Paulla motioned for us to descend. We had no choice: the thought of going back the way we had come, up onto the main deck, into the arms of the Pirate Admiral, was too terrifying.

Slowly, letting our feet search out each step, easing our weight from leg to leg, we passed to the deck below. It was an oar deck, and dark but for the dim moonlight peeking in from the oar ports in the ship's sides. The ceiling was no more than four feet high. I expected the snoring and stench of the rowers, the shuffle of chains, but instead we felt the stillness of hollow, empty space. The quinquereme was shorthanded, and the pirates had kept this uppermost bank of oars unmanned.

"Ow, oh," came a sudden moan, right at our feet, followed by a sigh and sniffle. By the faint moonlight we could just discern that a man was lying sprawled across our path.

Paulla, in front, did not hesitate. She crouched at the figure's head, lifted her hand, and knocked the man's head with the bronze lamp. There was an exhalation of breath and another deep sigh.

"Step carefully!" she whispered.

"Was that in *The Twice-Told Tale* too?" I asked.

"I'm improvising," came the soft response.

Gingerly, stooping beneath the low deckhead, we stepped across the drunken pirate. I actually trod on his fingertip and had to catch myself against the beam to pull the weight off my foot at the last moment, but the pirate's breathing never altered.

The noises of the ship echoed eerily down the long, empty deck. As we picked our way between the oars (which were drawn inboard), the slightest scuff of our sandals seemed ten times magnified, and more than once we all froze in terror, certain that the pirates must have heard us. In turn, we could hear the rumble of the Pirate Admiral's curses as he plotted strategy with his companions. From farther forward came echoes of drunken revelry – the pirates had plundered Pompey's supply depot on Samos and were eating and drinking it all up. Beneath all of that was a low rumble, the snoring of two hundred slaves. Somewhere among them, I knew, was our dear Captain, but there was no hope of finding him there without being discovered ourselves.

At last we reached midships. There, an oar had been removed and the oar port was open. I put my head out the side and saw the *Hesiod* floating a short distance away. There were no lights aboard. The little galley was perhaps thirty feet farther forward. Willing ourselves to go on, we reached a point we supposed must be level with the *Hesiod*'s stern.

"We'll have to use one of the oars," I said quietly. "Lower it. Crawl down."

Paulla nodded. Homer did not.

"Sir, I must remind you that I can't swim!" he whispered loudly.

"What do you mean?" I asked. "Keep your voice down!"

"I mean, sir, that I had to use the bladder when we were shipwrecked! I am unable to swim!"

"What do you do at the baths?" I whispered back.

"I luxuriate, sir! In the hot, shallow pool!"

"Don't worry, Homer," said Paulla softly. "Marcus and I will pull you, all right? But don't splash, they'll hear it!" She pointed upward.

Homer clearly thought it was lunacy, which did give me pause for thought, but how else could we reach the *Hesiod*? Gently, we lifted an oar – it took all three of us, straining, to ease it up – and let it slide down, inch by inch, to the water. Its blade gave a gentle plop and then floated up, the shaft wedged at an angle into the oar port.

"I'll go first," whispered Paulla. She hitched up her dress and ducked through the narrow opening. Then, wrapping her ankles and elbows around the shaft, she began to descend.

"All right?" I asked Homer. He shivered, but agreed. I followed after him as soon as I heard the soft gurgle of Paulla sinking into the water by the oar blade.

By Hercules, Homer took that oar slowly. You would never have called him athletic, but he certainly was methodical. He crept down, ankles clenched, as if his life depended on it, which in fact it did. My muscles were burning and my joints were aching by the time I joined them in the cold water of the bay. Gripping Homer by the collar, Paulla and I dragged him the short distance between the two ships, paddling with our limbs beneath the surface and with barely a sound to indicate our passage.

Overhead loomed the stern of the *Hesiod*, far lower than the giant quinquereme. Still, its slick sides offered no grip for climbing hands. Instead, we had to feel our way down the length of the port side, with the *Hesiod* to hide us from the quinquereme, up to the ram at the bow. The pirate boarding-party had drawn in the oars, but our Athenian rowers were long gone. As we listened for sounds of life on board the galley, we heard nothing. The ram furnished just the extra few feet we needed to grab hold of the rail. Together, Paulla and I hauled Homer up.

Shivering now, we crouched on the boarding deck, covered by the ballista. The *Hesiod* was well and truly deserted. The pirates were badly undermanned, and a twenty-oar galley was evidently not worth guarding. But they had taken all the stores.

"We'll have to use the sail," I told Paulla. "But just a sliver of it, mind. We have to keep it quiet, we can't outrun anybody. Three feet at most. Loosen the halyards and I'll cut the anchor."

By now, we were a competent crew. I headed for the stern and loosened the knot on the anchor cord. This seemed to take forever, but I had no knife to cut it free and we could never pull the anchor in without crashing it against the side.

At last the knot was free. The rope slipped and the *Hesiod* began to drift slightly. "Anchor away!" I called softly.

Homer and Paulla let the yard drop just a few feet. At once we began to move forward. There was a faint lapping of water at the bow.

"Shorten it!" I called.

We slowed to a steady glide. I took the steering oar. A light wind was blowing from the island, directly off the starboard beam, and this made our first progress rather slow. With one trireme still blocking the rear, we would have to curve around to the left, across the bow of the second trireme. Then we could run with the wind. I warned my crew to be ready to shorten sail again, and began the long, steady turn through the pirate fleet.

A burst of merriment and song shook the night. It came from inside the second trireme. Its crew was apparently more drunk than the crew of the quinquereme. I gave it as wide a berth as I could and then headed for the mouth of the bay.

The *Sword of Cilicia* was now behind us, and the drunken trireme nearly past. We were still going at a snail's pace. I had to alter course again to get past a small bireme, and still there was no sign that we were noticed. The night was thick enough, but surely someone must wonder about the little galley separating itself from the fleet?

At last we passed the final pirate vessel. The wind grew stronger as we neared the mouth of the bay. Paulla and Homer let the sail down to halfway and the water hissed as we picked up speed. The lights of the galleys behind us were fading now, lost in the distant lights of Samos.

My crew bounded up to the steering oar.

"Marcus, well done!" cried Paulla, wrapping her arms around me. Then she grabbed Homer by the shirt and shook him with excitement. "We did it, you crazy Greek, we did it! The *Hesiod* is ours!"

Homer was grinning with relief. "It is something, isn't it, to have stolen the same galley twice?"

"It is indeed," I agreed. "Especially when that galley's as fine a ship as this."

Once we had calmed down, we discussed a course. Homer pointed out that the pirates would certainly sail around the eastern end of Samos, between the island and the great headland of Mount Mycale, if they were making for Miletus; consequently, we should steer clear of that. Rather we might retrace our steps along the north coast of the island and from there swing south and east.

"But what if we come too late?" argued Paulla. "We have to tell Pompey about the pirate attack!"

"We do have a good head start," I countered. "Half the pirates will have headaches tomorrow. They can't reach Pompey until the day after, surely?"

In the end we agreed on Homer's course. None of us wished to have a pirate fleet on our trail, and we might still reach Miletus in time to warn Pompey. No one had the courage to mention the Captain, but we could all imagine him there, somewhere in the flagship. It was heartbreaking to see his cushions still lying scattered about the poop deck.

Our main problem was navigation. None of us had sailed to Miletus before, and the pirates had stolen the Captain's charts. We knew, from our outward voyage, that we would have to find the channel south between Corassia and Samos, but from there our only idea was to go vaguely south-east.

Homer, of course, volunteered to navigate. He claimed to have memorized his versified astronomical treatise, and he knew the constellations as we headed west with a good backing breeze. We sighted Mount Kerketeus before dawn, its peak of white chalk glimmering faintly in the moonlight; this marked the western end of the island. We steered south about its feet. As the light grew, we could tell we had come too close to the archipelago of Corassia, and we veered south-east.

Then the wind died. It had carried us west alongside Samos and nearly to the open sea, but by mid-morning we lay becalmed. The square-rigged sail drooped from the yardarms, try as we might to stiffen it. The sky was free of cloud in every direction, save for a little pile off the tip of Kerketeus, still visible to the north-west. Another galley might have rowed its way onward, but the *Hesiod* had no such choice.

Noon came and the afternoon dragged on. I slept in the cabin, telling Paulla to wake me if we moved, but when I opened my eyes again at dinnertime, I found that nothing had changed, except that we were all powerfully hungry and had nothing to eat. Homer tried praying to various wind gods, but either he misremembered the poems they preferred or they were busy elsewhere, blowing against a different galley's sail.

"Look at it this way," I told Paulla, who had not stopped pacing and looking at the eastern horizon. "The pirates sail by the same winds as we do, don't they?"

"They're not *sailing* at all," she replied. "They're rowing." And I had to stop her from wasting her strength at an oar herself.

At last, at dusk, a wind swept down from Mount Kerketeus. The sky was still clear, but the high airs were flowing fast. Perhaps a storm was brewing. Regardless, we adjusted the angle of the sail and soon were speeding south-east through the lowering night.

Here Homer's constellations failed us. He claimed that he had not studied that part of the astronomical treatise that dealt with the south-east at that time of year, and he began mistaking one set of stars for another, muttering verses under his breath all the while.

"Confound it," he whispered to himself, "is it *the red star sunk beneath the belt*, or *beside* the belt? Which is the belt? The *thrice-bejeweled belt* or the one with four? More that way, sir!"

"Starboard?" I asked.

"Yes, indeed, starboard. Does that look like a *thrice-bejeweled* belt to you, sir? Or would you say it's more *wan beneath the weight of heaven*?"

So much for the science of astronomy, I thought, and gave up wondering where we were. I knew that if we kept sailing we must reach civilization eventually, but how long could we last without food?

Paulla's keen eyes saw it first.

"Marcus," she said, hurrying back to the steering oar. She looked extremely tired. "Do you see that light over there?" She pointed through the night.

"Off the port side?" I asked nautically.

"Right, over there, just by the sail. Isn't that light, or are my eyes playing tricks?"

By Hercules, it was light indeed – a minute point of light that was not a star. It was some miles away to the north, as best I could reckon – certainly not the great city of Miletus, but it might save us. We veered round, as close to the wind as we could, and after half an hour we could tell it was actually a cluster of lights above the line of the horizon.

"It must be an island," I said, "but I can't see any land. We should slow down."

Coming closer, we discovered that the land was all too near. We were entering a broad bay, half a mile across, which split into three smaller bays. The light was coming from the hillside at the back of the largest of these, in the middle.

"Must be a village," Paulla said, and went to wake Homer, who had given up navigating in favor of sleep. The two of them searched the hold for something heavy and found a sack of rusty iron. Tying this to a length of rope, they made a new anchor. Meanwhile, the galley crept past the mouth of the bay and drew toward the steep hillside. I brought us in as close as I thought safe.

"Lower the sail!" I called.

"Sail down!" returned Paulla, loosing the halyards.

"Anchor away!" I called.

Homer dropped the anchor over the side. It struck bottom rather quickly. I was relieved to find that he had first attached one end of the rope to the galley.

We agreed that Homer, who dreaded another encounter with the sea, would stay and guard the galley while Paulla and I swam to shore and explored.

We dove over the side with a splash. The bay was slimy and thick with seaweed, but we managed to get ashore in the dark. I had forgotten that Paulla was such a strong swimmer. At the end of the bay we found a short pier, but we could see no boats tied up alongside. The hillside rose steeply from the beach, and from where we stood we could no longer see the yellow light.

"There must be a path," remarked Paulla, and sure enough we found one at the end of the pier. It went up in short zigzags, just gentle enough for a donkey to climb. After we had reached the second turn, we heard a burst of merry song from the village above – and the sound of a drum.

"Is it Greek?" I asked.

"I can't tell," whispered Paulla. "We should be careful."

"Why, yes, it is one of our favorite songs," said a man's voice, in Greek, from close by.

We spun around, but there was no one there.

"I'm above you! Hello! Look up!" called the voice again. "It's a steep path. Hold on, we shall come down to you!"

A moment later, two men came jogging down the path and turned the corner above us. They were wearing sheepskin coats and were clean shaven. On their heads they wore broad, flat-brimmed hats. Each of them had a dagger at his waist, but their hands were spread in welcome.

"Strangers!" cried one of them, an older man with gray hair. "Welcome to our little island! It is long since anyone came across the wine-dark sea to us." The men reached us and clasped my hand firmly in theirs. When they noticed that Paulla was a girl, they took off their hats and bowed. Then they presented us each with a gift of welcome – one pear each. These were round, glossy, and firm.

"Thank you," I replied self-consciously.

"We heard the splashes in the bay," said the younger man eagerly. "And we thought you were seeking refuge from the storm."

"Storm?" I asked.

"There will be a storm tonight," replied the older man. "And then it will be a night indeed. *Now keep no ships upon the wine-dark sea . . .*"

". . . *but surely stick to land, as I decree,*" finished the younger man. They both laughed. "Not bad, eh, stranger? Of course, one expects good advice from the poet."

"The poet?" I asked sharply.

"Hesiod, sir, the prince of poets," replied the old peasant gravely. "Very well put, wouldn't you say?"

A lunatic thought crossed my mind. "Kind sirs," I began, "may I inquire as to the name of this island?"

"This island, stranger? Why, have you no chart, or has it been so long that the world has forgotten us? You have reached the island of Tragias, my friend, famous for its pears. And rightly so, as you can . . . But where is she going?" he cried in alarm.

Paulla had given me her pear, turned right round, and bolted down the path. The peasants looked at me in astonishment as she disappeared into the darkness.

"Why," exclaimed the young man, "surely that's rather unfair. How can we have such a bad reputation, when no one ever comes here?"

We stood in uncomfortable silence. A splash from below, magnified by the encircling hills, indicated that Paulla had jumped into the water again and was swimming back to the *Hesiod*. I munched my pear, which was indeed delicious. The peasants strained their ears. There came the sounds of a struggle aboard the ship. Homer was protesting. Then we heard a tremendous splash, followed by cries for help, and another, gentler splash as Paulla dived in after him.

Some moments afterwards, Homer and Paulla rounded the turn below us. The publisher was trailing seaweed, but as they approached I noticed a faraway look in his eyes.

"Is this really Tragias?" he asked.

"Yes indeed, sir," replied the old peasant. "Have you heard of it?"

Homer answered nothing at first. Then, with tears, he began to sing softly:

> When the wind is from the empty sea
> The pear tree blossoms blow
> Across the only land and hills
> That I shall ever know.

The peasants gaped at him, thunderstruck, and then roared. Then they threw their arms about him.

"You must be from Tragias," cried the old man. "But who are you? We don't know you!"

"You knew me as a boy, Megacles," Homer answered. "My name was Menedemeroumenos."

"Menedemeroumenos?" cried the old man. "*Little* Menedemeroumenos, the son of Dionosoupatros? But you were taken by the pirates!"

"Menedemeroumenos?" I asked, turning to Paulla. "Seriously?"

"Yes, they took me," said Homer. "But now I'm back. Let us go up to the village."

The two peasants insisted on carrying Homer on their shoulders the rest of the way, shouting all the while. This was quite difficult and took some time, since the path was so steep. When we got there we found that somehow, as if by magic, the news had spread through the village that a long lost citizen of Tragias had returned. They had already been engaged in a village dance – that was the light we saw at sea – but something new had been hastily organized. When we appeared, the young girls all burst into song and started running in a circle round the village altar, while a second ring of boys danced around them, and the grown men and women clapped time. Everyone was singing.

Homer stood in the glow of the torches, taking it all in. Every moment brought a new look of recognition and he smiled at a face in the crowd. The song ceased with a flourish of uplifted hands, and then, as one, the people surged toward him. We stood aside and watched an old man with a long beard, the Chief Magistrate of Tragias, make his way forward. He embraced Homer and held up his hand for silence.

"Menedemeroumenos, the son of Dionosoupatros, has returned!" the Magistrate now proclaimed.

The crowd roared its approval. Homer whispered something in his ear.

"And he has changed his name to Homer!" the magistrate added.

Another enormous burst of approval from the crowd.

"And he is now a Roman citizen!"

At this the villagers murmured happily. It must have been incredible that a citizen of that small community could be a Roman, a member of that distant, powerful nation they must often have heard of but had certainly never seen. Yet they took it as quite natural.

At this point the throng of villagers parted before another figure. It was an old woman, somewhat stooped, wearing a knitted red shawl across her shoulders. She shuffled forward to where Homer stood and looked at him keenly. Without a word he knelt in front of her and she kissed his forehead.

I pressed forward to meet her. She looked at me kindly.

"Are you – are you Homer's mother?" I stammered.

She seemed somewhat deaf and did not hear. Homer repeated the question in her ear and she looked at me and smiled again. Homer answered for her.

"Not my mother, sir, I'm afraid. This is my great aunt by marriage. This, dear Great Aunt, is Marcus Oppius, a noble Roman."

"He seems a bit young!" she said hoarsely.

"But where is your family, Homer?" I asked. "Where are your mother and father?"

"Taken! They were all taken!" croaked the old woman, hearing me this time. "The pirates took them away. Never saw them again, no, except for dear little Menedemeroumenos!"

"It's Homer now, Great Aunt," said Homer quickly.

But her response struck a chord in me. I felt the breath of inspiration upon my forehead. On the spur of the moment, I seized a stool and stood tall amid the crowd. Seeing me, they fell silent, unsure of what I intended.

"Citizens of Tragias!" I began, haltingly. It was time to make a speech – a real speech. Nothing could hold me back.

"Citizens of Tragias! I come to you as a companion-in-arms of your long lost Mene . . . of your long lost Homer! But we did not sail here to the island of Tragias, deservedly famous for its pears, with the purpose of bringing him to you. No, it was only luck, and the will of the gods, that he should be restored to you, and you should be restored to him. How could the gods bear it, that so famous a man and so famous an island should be parted forever? Now that I myself have seen Tragias, I realize that all those noblest qualities I have come to respect and admire in him" – spare me, Jupiter, the dire penalties of perjury – "such as modesty, humility, and self-sacrifice, are all to be found on the isle of Tragias itself!"

Great applause at this: I was clearly speaking the truth.

"There is a time for celebration, my friends. There is a time for tears. There is a time for thanking the everlasting gods. But there is also a time for vengeance!"

I had said the right thing. Vengeance was clearly one of the more popular activities on Tragias. The crowd was firmly of my opinion.

"Only last night," I continued, "we escaped from our enemies, the Aegean pirates. They boarded us and planned to use our ship against Rome. They held us captive. Even now, one of our comrades lies dying at the pirate oars."

A sympathetic murmur from the people here, and one of the women put her arm around Paulla. Someone cursed the pirates angrily.

"Even now," I went on, "the pirate fleet is sailing to Miletus, where they will dare to confront the power of Rome. The pirates wish to continue their pillagings, their depredations. But Rome will not allow it! We will not allow it! How many islands have they not despoiled? The proof of it is here, on Tragias itself. I ask the pirates, why are there empty homes? Where is the lost family of Menedemeroumenos?"

I managed the name. They were cheering every sentence now. I headed for the homestretch.

"Come with us tonight, citizens of Tragias! Join with Rome against the pirates, as you joined with Athens against the Persians, as you joined with Achilles against the Trojans! This very hour, we are sailing to attack the pirates. They have wronged me. They have wronged Tragias. And most of all, they have wronged your Menedemeroumenos!"

The crowd erupted with cheers. Homer was picked up and passed across the sea of arms. But I knew I needed one more line.

"We did not sail to Tragias," I proclaimed, "but Tragias will sail with us!"

The roar was deafening. Then the crowd scattered, rushing home for their weapons. A dozen village elders ran up to press my hand and kiss me on both cheeks. In no time, the citizens of Tragias returned in mode of war. Spears and swords bristled in every man's hand. Paulla was at my side, looking rather beautiful, her eyes shining.

I will never forget that march in triumph down the steep path to the bay. Homer was at the front, reveling in the glory of Tragias; the hills echoed with enthusiastic battle cries. As we descended, more villagers sought me out in the line to praise my speech. They also took the opportunity, in low voices, to offer hints of constructive criticism, mainly about my failure to quote Hesiod (which was customary), and on some of the grammatical constructions I had employed, which were not necessarily in the best taste.

The stars were veiled as we set forth, covered by a storm-bank of cloud. The little *Hesiod* was filled to bursting with armed men, two for each oar and many more on the boarding deck, waiting their turn. Paulla was instructing four of them in the use of the ballista. All through the last hours of the night, across heaving seas, we made up for lost time. No galley in the world could have outpaced us. We were bound for Miletus. Every mind was intent on vengeance. Every heart ached for battle.

12

The Battle of Miletus

All night the *Hesiod* struggled against the stormy sea. But the gods kept the rain back, even if the booming thunder seemed to come from right overhead. Everyone was soaked with spray. Each tall crest of water was a new challenge to the rowers, as the galley fought its way up the rising slopes and came tearing down again. The west wind blew with frightening power, so that I had to hold on to the poop-deck rail with one hand and call someone to help me with the steering oar.

Having chosen their course of action, the fifty men of Tragias never faltered. The knowledge that our galley was named the *Hesiod* went a long way in sustaining them. After the first shift of rowers, I was surprised to find the Chief Magistrate joining me on the poop deck. In spite of his age, he had insisted on joining the expedition and on taking the first shift at the oars. His wrinkled eyes were full of fire.

He seemed to regard me as the man in charge. Answering my question, he declared that it was seventeen miles from Tragias to Miletus. He had often made the trip in his youth, trading pears on the mainland, but lately the risk of being taken by pirates had ruined all commerce. Many citizens of Tragias, I learned, had been captured on this stretch of sea, besides those seized from their homes during the pirates' coastal plunderings.

He was just giving me a description of the harbor when our conversation was interrupted by Homer. The publisher was looking brave, but fairly seasick.

"Sir, if I may make a suggestion . . ." he began.

"You may indeed," I answered grandly.

"It is about the *Hesiod*. The hull, sir, and the sail. I took the liberty, while my fellow citizens were running for their weapons, of bringing two pots of paint from the village. Red and yellow, to be precise."

"To throw in the faces of the pirates, you mean?"

"Hardly, sir. I was thinking that we should decorate ourselves *as* a pirate – a pirate ship, that is. You know, sir, gaudy colors and so forth."

I grasped his idea. Paint would hardly fool the pirates up close, but from a distance we might well be mistaken for a pirate trireme. Perhaps it could buy us time. Most of all, it might sow confusion. The only problem was that the house from which Homer had taken the paint was the Chief

Magistrate's own. I had to assure the old man that Rome would amply compensate him, assuming we survived.

So, amidst the rolling waves, Homer set to work with his pots of paint, assisted by half a dozen men. For the hull we chose a simple pattern of vertical stripes: as Homer remarked, it was both tasteless and fearsome, which was just what we were looking for. On the sail, Homer painted the emblem of Medusa's Head, with red snakes writhing from the monster's skull and long yellow fangs. Nothing, he remarked with satisfaction, could be less Roman. In the end there was only a little paint left.

"Don't waste it on any more stripes," Paulla advised. "Why don't we paint red dots on the foreheads of half the crew, yellow dots on the other half? If it comes to close fighting, Marcus, we might need to know who's on our side."

She supervised the painting of dots on the men of Tragias, who thought it was great fun and immediately began making up songs about the glory of the red dots and the courage of the yellow. Paulla herself painted me with the last yellow dot.

A dull dawn came at last, three hours out from Tragias. As the light increased, we could see the mainland before us like a band of gray haze. We were right on course. The wind grew less intense.

Paulla joined me at the steering oar. "I'm actually a little nervous about the battle, Marcus," she confessed. "Not because of Aulus – he can take care of himself, you know – but because of the Captain. What happens if we start sinking pirate ships, and he's chained to an oar? I don't want him to drown!"

Of course she was right, and I reassured her that we would not ram the pirates directly. For one thing, fast as we were, I doubted if the *Hesiod*'s bronze-covered ram would do much damage to a trireme, much less the great *Sword of Cilicia*.

"In any case," I added, "I'm hoping there won't *be* a battle. If we can warn Pompey in time, he can escape."

"I hope you're right, Marcus."

We were now coming up on Lade Island. This was a long, tall, forested hunk of land just west of Miletus. The ancient city itself was built on a peninsula that jutted far into the Latmian Gulf. A mist lay on the morning waters.

"Can you see anything?" I asked Paulla, who was gazing at the harbor with her keen eyes. She had tied her hair back into a bun; and was shielding her gaze against the rising sun.

"I think there are ships on the far point of the island," she said. "There's something moving in the mist."

"We'll have to be careful," I said. "No more sailing into the pirate fleet and knocking on the front door."

I summoned the Chief Magistrate from his oar.

"Can a ship pass between Lade Island and the peninsula?" I asked him. "I don't want to be seen as we come round the island."

The Chief Magistrate frowned at the idea. "That channel's not very deep," he declared. "More silt every year, coming down the river. No big ship would try it."

That decided me. The *Hesiod* had a very shallow draft, and no one would be expecting a galley to squeeze through. We would attempt it. I steered for the gap between Lade and the mainland.

The channel was a mile long. When we reached the mouth of it, we could suddenly see past the forested slopes of Lade. As Paulla had guessed, there were indeed many galleys beyond, though they were not in the harbor. Some clearly belonged to the pirates: the giant quinquereme that served as the Pirate Admiral's flagship, for one, with four triremes in line behind it. They were circling from left to right, then reversing direction. Away to the north was a squadron of pirate biremes, performing a similar maneuver.

By the time we were halfway through the channel, we could tell what they were doing. Four Roman triremes were trapped between the pirate fleet and the peninsula of Miletus. Now I saw why both sides' ships had been difficult to discern. They had taken down their sails and masts. Battle had been joined.

Outnumbered, the Romans had assumed the "wheel" formation, each ship aligned with a central point, prows facing outwards. This prevented the pirates from ramming them amidships, while if the enemy tried to attack head-on, into the teeth of the Roman rams, both ships would be shattered. It was a desperate defensive tactic, but the alternative was swift destruction.

The Pirate Admiral, for his part, was countering this with the "roundabout" tactic, trying to edge his galleys around the rim of the Roman wheel formation and thus force the Romans closer and closer together. When he had succeeded on one end of the "wheel," he would turn his ships and sail around the other end, forcing it back in turn, all the while using the squadron of biremes to protect his flank. Soon we could hear the *wham*s of the ballista bolts being launched by both sides, as well as the crunches when they struck enemy hulls. The pirates were cheering, trying to goad the Romans galleys out to sea; if they refused, the Pirate Admiral's encircling tactics would gradually drive our friends against the rocks of the peninsula.

News of the battle spread swiftly down the *Hesiod*. Our men began to chant an old war song of Tragias, until Paulla told them to be quiet. We hoisted Homer's sail, with its Medusa's Head, to show that we were fellow pirates, and Homer coached the rowers in a cheer of "Up with Red Beard! Down with Pompey!" All the while we were tearing up to the battle. The citizens of Miletus were on the shore, watching the struggle in the bay.

Surely everyone could see us now. But perhaps the pirates were preoccupied. Just as we passed through the channel (with a near-miss scrape of our bottom at the far end), two pirate triremes moved in against the wheel formation. One dashed for an unprotected Roman side, all oars churning wildly. But the Roman captain saw it in time and smartly backed off, facing the pirate trireme. I saw that the Roman prow was decorated with red and white checks: it was none other than the *Rapacious*, the warship that had carried Spurinna to Greece. Suddenly it was the pirates' turn to avoid being rammed, and with a fountain of foam, their oars backed water and retreated.

Another Roman ship was not so lucky. The pirate trireme, its rails sparkling with gold paint, seemed willing to ram head-on, and it tore straight toward the smallest of the Roman galleys. Just as we braced ourselves for the crack of impact, however, the pirate swerved aside. Long poles were lifted from its sides and dangled over the Roman galley. Their ends seemed to be smoking.

"Fire pots!" cried Homer in dismay.

So indeed they were. To the ends of the poles, the pirates had fastened clay jugs of flaming pitch. When they let the poles fall, the jugs smashed on the Roman deck, covering it with inextinguishable flame. Thick black smoke rose up. Soon we could see flames leaping high from the inside. The pirates gave a mighty cheer as the Romans leaped overboard from the burning trireme.

"How can we get in?" asked Paulla. "They're down to three ships now! They need our help!"

"You mean, how can we get in and die with them?" I asked. "Forget it. We have no choice but to attack!"

At my command, Homer and his painting crew took down the sail and began to dismantle the mast. We sped toward the heart of the pirate fleet, which was racing around the Roman flank once again. This time, they were trying to cut off the largest Roman galley, presumably Pompey's flagship. Taking notice of us at last, however, one pirate trireme detached itself and moved in our direction.

"Get ready with that cheer!" I called.

The pirate trireme cut toward us. It was at least four times our size, with one hundred and fifty oars lifting and pulling in unison. Still, it seemed unsure of who we were and did not accelerate to ramming speed.

"Now, Homer!" I shouted.

On cue, our fifty crewmen cried, "Up with Red Beard! Down with Pompey! Hurrah! Hurrah! Hurrah!"

The enemy slowed sharply. I could see curious faces looking down from the pirate bow.

"Ramming speed!" I shrieked.

I jammed the steering oar to one side. The rowers redoubled their efforts, throwing their full strength into the frantic tempo. Paulla was calling the beats. It felt like we were literally flying over the water.

"Cease rowing! Starboard oars up!" I commanded.

The rowers lifted their oars and heaved them high in the air, bracing their shoulders against them.

"Heads down! This is it!"

The *Hesiod* was pointed like a ballista bolt along the enemy's starboard bank of oars. Nothing could have turned us. It was too late to evade. Our bronze-covered ram went straight down the forest of oar shafts like a thunderbolt. We heard countless cracks and tearings and splinterings as oar after oar was broken in half.

"Now we turn and board them?" cried Paulla.

"No! Full speed ahead!"

Using our own oars, which had survived unhurt, to shove off from the crippled pirate ship, we cleared the wreckage of the enemy side and swiftly passed to its rear. It tried coming after us, but with only half its propulsion intact, it could only turn in circles. Our crew, drenched in spray, couldn't resist giving them one last farewell.

"Up with Red Beard! Down with Pompey! Hurrah! Hurrah! *Hurrah!*" they shouted gleefully.

Meanwhile, the pirates were bearing down once more upon the *Rapacious* and Pompey's flagship. With horror, we watched as the *Sword of Cilicia* rammed the Roman admiral's galley, catching it just before the prow. It wasn't a damaging blow, but the two ships were now locked together. A horde of pirates was gathering on the quinquereme's boarding deck, intent on slaughter.

The *Rapacious* was caught between two fires. That is, two pirate triremes faced it, and as soon as it spun its bow round to fend off the first, the second would maneuver to ram from the side. It was twisting this way and that, backing water all the while. The shore was all too near.

"Switch shifts, now!" I called. "Fresh rowers! Quickly, quickly!"

The men of Tragias exchanged places on the benches, and fresh backs and biceps took control. The others looked to their weapons, Paulla went forward to direct the ballista, and Homer joined me.

"Sir, we must save that Roman!" he said, pointing to the *Rapacious*.

"I know," I replied. "We'll have to wait till the last moment – timing, Homer, timing is everything!"

We were about a hundred yards from the *Rapacious*. One of the pirate triremes veered to ram, but without momentum, and the *Rapacious* was able to evade. But this left it exposed to the other pirate galley, which backed water, lining up with the Roman ship's side.

"Don't they see us?" I asked Homer.

Half a dozen ballista bolts answered my question. Both pirate galleys had us in their sights. Several missiles struck home among our rowers, and another barely missed Paulla at the bow.

"Fill their places!" I ordered. "Prepare to ram!"

Once more, we accelerated across the sea. We were coming in at an angle behind the pirate that was backing water. But we were far faster. In moments, we had come level with the enemy prow.

"Port oars only!" I shouted. "Port oars only!"

The *Hesiod* turned very sharply. I wondered if we would capsize. Then, suddenly, we came out of the turn and were flying toward the pirate bow.

"Both sides! Both sides! Ramming speed!"

The fresh strength of Tragias gave six quick pulls of the oars and we impacted on the pirate ram. Our own bronze ram struck it right where it joined the trireme hull. There was a sickening lurch and an ear-splitting crack, and the pirate ram was sheared off as if by a chisel.

"Starboard oars up!"

In the nick of time, the *Hesiod* lifted the ten starboard oars, passing directly under the shattered pirate bow. The enemy was still afloat, but without its ram it would be quite unable to attack.

A tremendous cheer went up from the *Rapacious*. Then the Roman galley turned against the first attacker, beating it back and threatening to strike in turn.

Now we were fifty yards off from Pompey's flagship. Shouts and cries and the scrape of metal reached us from the point where the quinquereme had dug itself into the Roman ship: a ferocious mêlée was underway as the Romans fought back the pirate boarding party.

"That's it!" I shouted to Homer. "That's the battle now!"

I changed course toward the stern of the *Sword of Cilicia*. My face was flushed with the joy of our first successes. It was so much more satisfying to maneuver the *Hesiod* with oars than to be always imploring the gods for a favorable wind. The steering oar felt like a toy in my hand.

The quinquereme loomed overhead. We were too low for the ballista bolts to hit us. In a few strokes we would reach the pirate hull.

"Ready your weapons!" I ordered. "Now for Rome! Now for Tragias!"

The oarsmen tugged with all their strength, accelerating one last time, and then the *Hesiod*'s ram smashed into the side of the pirate stern. We did hardly any damage – for the quinquereme was built of huge thick timber – but we were stuck. That was all we needed. The blood rushed to my head.

"Now for it!" I cried. "Everybody out, we're boarding her! Board her, board her!" But the men on the boarding deck were already following Paulla into the belly of the *Sword of Cilicia*. The others dropped their oars, seized their spears and swords, and clambered after them. Homer and I brought up the rear.

Inside, it was a shambles. There was a choice of going down to the lowest oar-deck or up a damaged ladder at the side. Sensibly, Paulla led them upward. She had no weapon, which meant she could use both her hands to climb.

To my astonishment, the first room we passed through was the very storage chamber in which we had been held prisoner. At least this enabled us to get our bearings.

"Marcus!" called Paulla. "Marcus, we must be right below the poop deck!" She was pushing back through the crew.

"Any sign of the pirates?" I asked.

"One or two, but they took to their heels when they saw us," she grinned.

"Let's go for the poop deck, then," I said. Then, to the men of Tragias: "Everybody with a red dot on your forehead, follow the lady! If you've got a yellow dot, stay with me!"

The red dots followed Paulla up the ladder to the main deck. The yellow dots came after me.

A strange sight met our eyes. The enormously long deck of the *Sword of Cilicia* was almost empty. All the pirates were concentrated on the boarding deck, where the Romans had apparently repelled them and stormed aboard. But then the Pirate Admiral had rallied his men, pushing the Romans off again, and the pirates had even reboarded Pompey's galley. In the process, a pocket of Romans, fighting madly near the foremast, had been cut off and surrounded. The pirates were now split between those attacking the pocket of Romans and those fighting their way onto the Roman flagship.

By the time I got up, Paulla's red dots had claimed the poopdeck and cut down the pirate colors. Some thirty pirates were advancing on us, leaving some twenty more to press against the Roman pocket. My yellow dots formed a wall of spears across the main deck, and the pirates were beginning to attack them with long pikes.

"Well done!" I cried to Paulla. "But we have to advance!

Put the red spears with my yellow ones and hold this end of the ship!"

She nodded and grabbed a short sword.

"Stay safe, by Hercules!" I cried. Then I turned to Homer. "Pick your ten bravest, Homer, and follow me. Make sure they have swords. We have to rescue those Romans by the mast!"

"But how can we get past those pikes?" he asked.

"We'll go beneath them!"

In no time he had pulled ten young fellows back from the line of spears. They followed after me down the ladder again and I searched in the near-darkness of the corridor for the same hatchway that had allowed us to escape. I knew there was an empty oar deck down there, and it ran the length of the ship.

Dropping one by one down the steep stairwell, swords in our hands, we ran along the aisle between the massive drawn-in oars. We had to crouch beneath the deckhead, half-deafened by the echo of the battle above us. I was in the lead. We passed midships and the mainmast, then found another stairwell, going up, at the foremast. From the hatchway above I could hear the clank and screams of combat, as well as a familiar voice.

"To me! Romans to me! For Pompey! For Rome!" it called. There was something simple and unselfconsciously heroic in the intonation.

"Spurinna!" I cried, flinging myself up the stairwell. The others dashed up behind.

We were in the midst of the Roman pocket, surrounded by a ring of pirates. Spurinna was leading ten men in a circle, back to back, and they were slashing with their swords; some of their comrades lay dead or dying at their feet. A crowd of ugly, laughing pirates looked on, grasping pikes. The pirates were being careful, taking their time, and every few seconds a pike would come lunging in to kill another Roman. Spurinna ducked one thrust just as I appeared.

He looked at me with complete and total astonishment.

"No time to explain!" I shouted. "Tell your men not to attack anyone with a red or yellow dot on his forehead! That's us!"

"Us?" he gasped. Then, to give him credit, he at once gave the order to his men.

"Now let's break out of here and push them back to the stern!" I cried. "I'll take the port side. Spurinna, you take the middle. Homer, you take the starboard side. All right?"

"Homer?" Spurinna was more amazed than ever. The Greek publisher had just climbed up the hatchway. He gave a quick bow.

"My dear former master!" called Homer. "I would be glad to recount just how we happen to be on hand, but I'm afraid, well, the battle –"

But at that moment I shouted "Rome and Tragias!" and we charged the pirate pikes.

The pirates were hardly less amazed than Spurinna that twelve swordsmen had appeared, as if by magic, as reinforcements. To be effective with long pikes, you need either superior numbers or extraordinary discipline, and now they had neither. We slashed past the sharp pike tips and then the pirates couldn't recoil far enough to stab back. They turned and fled aft.

But there Paulla's spearmen were waiting. The pirates drew up before them, turned back to us, withdrew again. Suddenly it was their turn to be encircled, pressed between Paulla's men and ours. An awful howl of fear went up. In their midst, towering bravely and trying to encourage them, I saw the Pirate Admiral.

His red beard was askew, and he was bleeding from a cut in his forearm. But the old ferocity was still blazing in his eyes.

I stepped forward. The Pirate Admiral recognized me.

"You see," I declared. "I spoke the truth. You should have killed us on the spot. Now we've tracked you down!"

"By Sabazius!" roared the Pirate Admiral.

"For Tragias!" I shouted.

"For Tragias!" came the cheer from the stern. Paulla was waving her sword, clapping the villagers on the back.

With a roar, we advanced against the beaten enemy. They threw down their weapons and crowded toward the rail. There, some falling, some leaping, the pirate crew tumbled into the sea. Only the Pirate Admiral remained, keeping even the fiercest men of Tragias back with his expert cutlass strokes. At last he stood at bay, encircled by a double ring of spears. He dropped his sword. I took pity on him and accepted his surrender. From behind us came the sounds of Pompey and his crew driving the pirate boarding party in rout from the Roman galley's bow.

Spurinna, meanwhile, was still in shock. He was shaking Homer's hand in disbelief. The publisher was quoting a well-chosen verse. When Paulla walked up to him his astonishment reached its peak.

"Aemilia Paulla?" he asked, opening his eyes wide.

"Hello, Aulus," she answered with a smile. She had a light cut across her leg but was otherwise looking very fine.

"How – how in the name of Hercules did you get here?"

"Oh, well, Marcus and I sailed to Greece, you see," she began.

I left them to it. Grabbing Homer, I hurried down the hatchway once more, then down a second hatchway to the middle oar deck. There I was met by a very frightened overseer. He took one look at me and fell on his knees with a shrill plea.

I realized I still had a sword in my hand. Also I was pretty much covered in blood, though thankfully unwounded. The overseer held up his whip to me in token of surrender.

"Get up!" I barked. "Where's the Captain? Have you been using this whip on him?"

I grabbed it from his limp hand and lifted it. But just

then there came a chorus of shouts from the stern. It was our captured Athenian rowers, chained to the oars, sitting together in a block.

"The Roman, the Roman!" they called. They were grinning with relief and delight.

I ran down to meet them. Homer followed, dragging the overseer behind him.

In the midst of the rowers sat a rather short, hefty figure with a great black beard. He was slumped over his oar, unconscious.

"Captain!" I cried. Then I turned with fury to the overseer. "Where are your keys? Release these men at once!"

He fumbled for the keys, and soon the freed Athenians were carrying the unconscious Captain up to the sunlight once more. Homer and I walked behind, not sure whether to grieve for the Captain's condition, or to be happy that he was still among the living. I felt more guilty than ever for having left him behind while we escaped.

On deck, there was silence, except for a single commanding voice. It belonged to a tall and handsome man with a narrow chin, wearing the armor of a Roman general. He was addressing the assembly of Roman sailors and men of Tragias. It was emphatically Pompey the Great himself.

". . . therefore I extend my thanks," he announced, "the thanks of the Admiral of the Mediterranean, to these men of Tragias, whose very surprising arrival so much assisted in this victory. From now on, let their island be known as

The Noble Island. Further, I can only praise this worthy Greek publisher, who captured the Pirate Admiral in personal combat. And last, but certainly not least, I salute my young protégé, ever in the forefront of the battle, who bravely routed the pirates almost single-handedly – Aulus Lucinus Spurinna."

There was a round of polite applause, sincere but futile protests from Spurinna (who was pointing at me), and admiration all round at the modesty of such a certifiable young Roman hero. The Chief Magistrate of Tragias went to ask for a lock of his hair.

Paulla ran up. With tears in her eyes, she stroked the Captain's beard where he lay on deck. Then she turned to me.

"Oh, Marcus," she said, "is he dead?"

But the Captain stirred. Opening one eye, he even managed a faint smile.

"You came back for me," he whispered softly. "You came back. Never, never, dear lady, have I seen such a wife, and such a husband, as you two, my dear friends." Then he passed out, and there was no time to correct him about me and Paulla.

Paulla gave orders for the Captain to be transferred to Pompey's flagship. No one thought to disobey. Then she stepped toward me and sank into my arms.

"The Captain's right, you know," she said. "You *are* the best, Marcus. I realized that just now, when you disappeared. Who cares about glory, if you're willing to be loyal to your friends?" She looked up, and suddenly there were tears in her eyes. "That's real love, isn't it, just like I told Zeno of Sidon?"

"It's not the kind you find in novels," I confessed.

She grinned and brushed her eyes. Suddenly, she kissed me.

"Marcus," she said, "it's the kind you find in your heart, when the gods are helping the brave. Now come on, and let's get over to the flagship. You're covered in blood, as you might have noticed."

Four of the pirate galleys were captured at Miletus, including of course the *Sword of Cilicia*. The rest scattered far and wide, pursued by the victorious Roman fleet. Pompey's flagship was too badly damaged to join the chase, however. The quinquereme's ram had left a huge gap in the hull, and it had to limp back to Athens. This suited Pompey well, for he was keen to return to Italy in triumph; but he dismissed Cicero's note (which was found on the *Sword of Cilicia*) and the alliance with Cicero never quite worked out. He took the Pirate Admiral with him, in chains.

Covered in glory, the men of Tragias went home, having lost five islanders in the battle; but they had already begun to compose an epic poem on the subject, with me as the principal hero. It is still, I'm sure, the only island of two hundred inhabitants with its own quinquereme floating in the bay. Homer did not go with them, though he promised to visit. He took up residence in Athens and began publishing Spurinna's memoirs. They were more in demand than ever.

Spurinna remained with the Roman fleet. They promoted him to be first officer of the *Rapacious*, a rather extraordinary post (it was remarked) for an extraordinary young man. He did shake my hand before he sailed. Somehow, he said, he seemed to have got all the credit I deserved.

"It's all right," I told him. "I'm not the hero type."

As for the Captain, he sailed with us to Athens. There, he was again treated by Atticus's doctor friend, and his leg mended slowly. Later he wrote to me from Carthage. He had sold the *Hesiod* to Atticus and bought a new merchant ship instead. His return home was a magnificent event, he declared, and his entire clan voted to put up a life-sized bronze statue of him – which, given the Captain's hefty physique, must have cost a small fortune.

Paulla and I went back to Rome – by land as much as possible. Her escape and her adventures were the scandal of the year in the City, and she reveled in every minute of it. Her parents, still enraged at her running away from home, forced her to renew her betrothal to me with the most solemn vows imaginable, which displeased her rather less this time around. Nowadays, her idea of a good book is a philosophical dialogue, and she is always trying to get her friends to read them, but I don't mind.

As for myself, when I returned, I was prepared for the most withering lecture from Gaius. After all, it had taken me six months to complete my mission, and most of that had been spent planting barley. Gaius, however, was more than satisfied that there would be no alliance between Cicero and Pompey, and he hosted a grand victory banquet for me; his only real disappointment was that the pirates hadn't won. Caesar depends on him more than ever, now.

It was Homer, as you might expect, who had the last word on our adventures. He wasn't coming back with me and Paulla, but he did walk out to the Dipylon Gate to wish us luck on the journey home. There he presented us with one of the very first copies of Spurinna's memoirs, rolled on a beautiful silver handle. He was very pleased with it. Yet he seemed reluctant to say farewell.

"I've been thinking, sir," he said at last, "have you considered writing an account of our trip to Greece?"

"Certainly not," I replied.

"I only ask," he went on, "because there does seem to be a growing interest in these, well, these romantic novels. Not as much interest as in Hesiod, of course, and rightly so; but still, I think there is money in it, and my copyists are nearly finished with the Spurinna book."

"Any title in mind, Homer?" asked Paulla mischievously.

"Well, madam, I was thinking perhaps *The Tale of the Gallant Publisher*, or maybe –"

"Homer," I interrupted severely, "you're not suggesting that *I* should write a Greek romance novel?"

"Well, sir, as you must admit, our adventures did present some similarities to that, ah – to that type of story. I mean, there was the shipwreck, and the plantation, and the pirates, and Tragias, and the battle, and the, well, the happy couple at the end. Really, sir, what could be more suitable?"

"Homer," I said, "you're mad. Deranged. Insane."

Nonetheless, we got out of there as quickly as we could.

Historical Note

The Ancient Ocean Blues is set in the years 63 and 62 BC. The main historical event is Pompey the Great's campaign against the Cilician Pirates; the chronology of this has been adjusted, however, as it actually took place four years earlier (67-66 BC). Julius Caesar's election as High Priest (*pontifex maximus*) took place in 63 BC, very much as described in the first two chapters, though the detail of the bread is speculation. Gaius Oppius was one of Caesar's most loyal henchmen: he would later write the history of Caesar's victory in the Civil Wars (49-45 BC). T. Pomponius Atticus was indeed Cicero's best friend and a long-time resident of Athens: a biography of him survives, along with a good deal of his correspondence with his famous friend. Zeno of Sidon and Anaxilaus of Larissa were real philosophers of the period; the latter was later banished from Rome by Augustus, apparently for practicing magic. The Aemilii Paulli were one of Rome's most aristocratic families, but apart from her name Paulla is not based on a specific historical character. Marcus, Homer, the Captain, Aulus, and Brasidas are invented, though the worlds of political intrigue, book publishing, maritime commerce, naval warfare, and plantation slavery that they inhabit have been depicted as faithfully as possible.

The ancient novels that remain to us date from 100 to 200 years after this book takes place, but it is supposed here that they reflect an earlier, perhaps less sophisticated tradition – amply endowed though they are with pirates, bandits, disguise, coincidence, shipwreck, and adventure. Readers interested in a real ancient novel might try *Chareas and Callirhoe*, by Chariton of Aphrodisias. For the previous adventures of Homer, Aulus, and Tullia, you might enjoy *The Roman Conspiracy*, by the author of this book, also available from Tundra: this is the "Spurinna memoir" often rescued by Homer in *The Ancient Ocean Blues*.

For more historical information, including maps of Marcus's and Paulla's travels, please visit www.ancient-oceanblues.com.

Acknowledgments

I would like to thank my family for their moral support while I was writing this book. Kathy Lowinger and Kathryn Cole were of great help in improving the text, and it has been a pleasure to work with their colleagues Catherine Mitchell, Alison Morgan, Pamela Osti, Melissa Reeve, and Lauren Bailey at Tundra Books. Many thanks especially to Terri Nimmo for the striking cover design. I first read the Greek novels in Wade Richardson's excellent course at McGill in the year 2001.

ALSO AVAILABLE BY JACK MITCHELL

The Roman Conspiracy

With the Roman Republic crumbling, Aulus Lucinus
Spurinna finds his own family's world turned upside
down. Together with his faithful servant, Aulus must travel
to the great city of Rome to seek help from his family's
Protector. But Rome is more dangerous than he could have
imagined: a conspiracy of ruthless aristocrats and bloodthirsty gladiators threatens the survival of the Empire, and
soon Aulus finds himself involved. Even with the friendship of the beautiful Tullia, Aulus faces deadly danger and
mystery at every turn. Who can help to save his family's
land? Who can be trusted with the future of Rome?

PRAISE FOR

The Roman Conspiracy

"The Roman Conspiracy is a good strong adventure
story in the tradition of Rosemary Sutcliff and Geoffrey
Trease, with lots of action, a likeable hero, a feisty girl
(who actually does most of the thinking as well as a
good deal of the acting), and an historical setting about
which the reader is unlikely to know a great deal."
– *CM Magazine*
Highly Recommended

"*The Roman Conspiracy* is a fast-paced adventure story
with interesting characters and interwoven plots."
– *Resource Links*
Recommended

"Mitchell's classical adventure rivals Caroline Lawrence's
The Roman Mysteries (Millbrook) or Jane Yolen's *Young
Heroes* series (Harper Collins). Raised by his aunt and
uncle, Aulus Spurinna wants more than anything to see
the great city of Rome. This wish comes true under
tragic circumstances when his uncle mysteriously
dies. . . . Fast-paced action, an authentic setting, and
realistic characterization all work together to make this
an exciting journey to the ancient world."
– *SLJ*

"Jack Mitchell's *The Roman Conspiracy* is a compelling drama that sweeps readers into [the] historical moment with great verve. He does this partly by choosing an outsider to tell the story. Like the reader, Aulus, a boy from the provinces, is seeking Rome and all its wonders for the first time. Mitchell also cleverly integrates historical details into this story. And the novel's well-drawn teen characters, particularly Tullia, definitely make the novel much more accessible to contemporary readers. . . . Mitchell is a good writer, and this book, like Karleen Bradford's Crusades novels, is a valuable contribution to Canadian-authored historical fiction."
– *Quill and Quire*

" . . . a marvelous tale with the forward drive of a chariot. . . . *The Roman Conspiracy* should find a place alongside books by such esteemed writers as Rosemary Sutcliff and Geoffrey Trease. Jack Mitchell is a welcome new voice in . . . writing for young people."
– *Bill Richardson*